BOJANA STOJČIĆ

KNIVES ALL BLADE

tales from the dark

Foreword

by Susan Richardson—

Author of *Things My Mother Left Behind* (Baxter House Editions), *Tiger Lily* (JC Studio Press), and *Smatterings of Cerulean* (Dark Winter Press, 2025)

I have my good days and my bad days. During the good ones, I'm like a knife all blade

Knives All Blade is a collection of stories that delivers exactly what the title promises, and so much more. As I experienced this collection, slicing sensations reverberated in my consciousness, every story slicing open a piece of my heart, my mind, slicing into the fabric of what I believed to be real. These are stories that cut you to the bone with each word, each image, every feeling. You are left with no membrane to cloud the vision, no eyelids to conquer the darkness, no choice but to look, to see.

There's nothing worse than cutting with a dull knife

Rest assured there are no dull knives in this collection. Stojčić's stories carve into the shadows of humanity with meticulous dexterity, and spill over with curiously inexplicable shades of pain that gleam, even in deepest darkness. These stories are the underbelly of life, of the psyche, the dirty and depraved corners of the human experience, all illuminated under the brilliant artistic microscope that is the mind of Bojana Stojčić.

everybody's busy slitting throats and maintaining edges

In *Knives All Blade*, you will find vast and complex examinations of every facet of the human condition, examinations of mental health, family, sex, depravity, guilt, loneliness, loss and grief. You will partner in a provocative probe into the indelible stains of humanity, finding yourself pushed up against the textures of thought and action that so many try desperately to hide or erase. You will be introduced to dark and startling realities that you never imagined; all of this explored with language and images that are undeniably breathtaking. When you read these stories, you will respond not only with your intellect and emotion, but viscerally, with your whole body.

it's the sharpened edge of the scalpel of grief that cuts the deepest, hurts the worst, leaving scars that are impossible to hide

With incredible craft, Stojčić holds a magnifying glass up to the most intricate and sometimes disturbing scars, examines the detail, the origin, finds the cracks, goes beneath. She makes it impossible to look away from what human nature tries, with desperate futility, to ignore; and she does this with such skill, you come away feeling exposed, yet somehow cleansed, free.

their loss weaved through the whole fabric of our lives, into everything we've become, everything we know

One of the things I have always loved about Bojana Stojčić's writing is how she approaches the complexities of living so fearlessly and faces it all with wide open eyes and heart. She shies away from nothing and offers the landscapes of her own brilliantly beautiful mind with an unapologetic fierceness, an inescapable tenderness, and a truly unique twist of intellect that you cannot help but be in awe of.

we come wrapped in a thick skin...you need to be damn skilled to peel it off

Knives All Blade is a collection in constant motion, offering constant surprises. With fierce expression and adept precision, Bojana Stojčić peels off that thick skin with a ferocious splendour only she can deliver. Each story is ripe with some of the most striking language and metaphor that you will ever experience. She shows that there is no limit to the power of language when wielded from the depths of a mind supremely skilled at slicing apart the boundaries erected to obscure the fabric of the human experience. With her exquisite writing, Stojčić proves that she is unafraid to stand on the edge of a blade, to feel the pain, to taste the blood, and to cultivate bold, brave, magnificently surprising and brand-new realities.

To all those gorgeous people who gave me words
when silence was the only thing I could offer in return

"I've had so many knives stuck into me, when they hand me a flower

I can't quite make out what it is. It takes time."

— Charles Bukowski, Screams from the Balcony: Selected Letters 1960-1970

Strong as Death

(And the Weak Suffer What They Must)

"It's weird. I always feel him in my stomach first."

"Who, Ms. Roberts?" my new shrink asks as I enter his impeccably furnished office, hand firmly around my waist.

"Someone I met—a salesman with a portable stall whose latest album 'All of Me' sold at least two copies—I still touch to him though he's dead. It's Paula."

"Paula, please sit down," sunken cheeks nod, elbows propped on the recliner arms, "the person you mentioned, is he really dead or dead for you?"

"What difference does it make? He's gone. They both are."

"Please go on."

His legs are stretched straight out in front of him, feet still on the ground. (Mine can't stop bouncing.) He watches me secure my braid with an elastic, bangs hiding my eyes like a sheepdog, folds his hands and listens.

" 'How do you like your coffee?' my husband asked when we met. Strong. As a heart attack, I thought. A drink that is weak lacks flavor. The last coffee he made me was tasteless, like his accusations"—I crack my knuckles—"and weak, like my defense."

"How do you feel about it?"

I mull over before answering. He opens his paper notebook—loves neat format and unique designs—and starts jotting down notes. He hasn't gotten to the point where he's ditched it for an electronic one. His pencil writes like a charm.

"How do I feel about it!" I repeat, making a statement out of the question, and look around—walls lined with bookcases, perfectly aligned binders on the desk, a peacefully green carpet, cut to fit the shape of the room. The doc's into dull-red pens and Rubik's cubes, married, two underage kids, family grinning on the porch. Bloodhounds too.

Why am I so stupid when others are so smart? I keep thinking...And these dreams I've been having, dreams of all sorts—no need to go into details, I'll say, just so you know, in my dreams I'm none the wiser. I clench my hand into a fist, feel my fingernails dig into my palm. "You have an easier question?"

He blinks. I continue.

"I've been sick for so long it seems like a lifetime." I let the coat slide off my shoulders and fall to the couch. "Like the salamander's tail, I guess, easily broken off at a weak spot...Is there anything more devastating than the heart that bleeds? Maybe only skull-exploding silence, like you couldn't care less if the Earth stopped moving and everything was swept away into the atmosphere"—I take a small globe from the coffee table, glancing down at all that blue, let it spin round and round and round and decide, like the roulette wheel— "cypress swamps, gators and whispers in between, a picture on a wall in an apartment that's not mine, and a desk in a conference room that's not his, plums and cellos, and a hand holding a dandelion and my dog he hated and a pretzel shop we loved and a flower garden we grew inside, and nothing else." I straighten up, inhale deeply. "I need evidence I'm *alive*"—exhaling—"feel the blood rushing through my veins instead of creeping round my arms, legs, groin."

The doc seems agreeable, the kind of guy who always chooses the same side of the plane when preselecting a seat— he knows it needs daily practice, though, like singing. I bet he was real good friends with the bus driver, trying to get to school with as little drama as possible. He likes to think he wasn't a teacher's pet—but he totally was. Used phrases like *that's dumb* when he was being rebellious. I wonder what he's writing down. (Tense, struggling to focus, depressed, likely to have sat close enough to the middle section to get homework help and close enough to the back to keep her edgy side intact.)

He could be making a to-do list—get baby carrots from the store, food for dogs, fire extinguisher manual, work on book—or doodling. Everything's possible on the blank pages.

"What proof do you need?"

His pants buzz, cutting into my thoughts. He ignores it, writes something on a piece of paper, looking as if focusing on the reason why he wants neater handwriting. (Mine's messy, so fucking hard to decipher.)

"Oh, rarely anything can be proved to exist, especially when your life's been reduced to nothing. You see, in my dreams...No, no, forget about my dreams. It's always been like this—you have to be slow not to see it. I never liked mythology. There are no Easter bunnies around the corner or guardian angels, and scary clowns and witches are real, very real."

He rubs his wrist where he had a watch a moment ago. "Why is there something rather than nothing?!"

"I hereby confirm you're damn right, doc!" I stand up, shooting across the room like not-so-impressed a cat, and lean against the wall. "I wish I could clear everything out," I say, hand swooshing through the air like a knife that wants to cut it into thin strips like a bell pepper, "begin with an empty head, empty pages, beds and shelves, letting back in only those with credentials. Focus—sorry, pal, but you're playing for another team. Reality—dismissed. Mice and men—not on the list either. Dreams—oh, what the hell! Make yourselves at home. The wind—come on in! The sun—you too, buddy. The clouds, the rain—yes, yes! And the moon"—I go back to my place and look up at the low ceiling—"always visible to someone, somewhere...Last but not least, His Majesty the ocean"—I cross my legs—"one would do for now."

"Sounds like a good start to me," he says lightly, scratching his droopy ear.

"It does, doesn't it?" I almost scream. "Just imagine! Zero gigabyte memory, no temptations, no pain to go through, no need for forgiveness, no need to love and stop loving, fight and stop fighting—a predictable future."

"Time heals," he's optimistic, but that's ok—it's his job.

"Bullshit!" I say bluntly, uncrossing my legs. "Time doesn't heal. History doesn't teach. They ought to look up to mothers and their daughters, never missing an I-told-you-so chance. What's the use? We're bound to lose anyway. What's the use of raising your voice when you're an underdog? What's the use of remembering romantic post-it notes on the fridge or starving together or the light brush of passion skittering up your skin once they're gone?"

"I know but—"

"But what?" I cut him off. "Tummies are full, secrets betrayed, moments forgotten, fidelity underestimated, fidelity

5

overestimated, people like a limp handshake, certified as unfit for trust, staying late at work. 'Go home already!'—you're told. What is home? Where is it? We are but singular stories—self-governed and incapable of shared destinies. Unloving and unlovable. God himself grew tired and retired. Why wouldn't we?"

I begin to cough. He indicates a glass of water with a jerk of his head. I drink some, lick my lips, then slow down.

"Spouses are experts at driving each other crazy, holding onto old grudges and waking up angry, longing for things out of their reach"—I gulp and fix my eyes on a burn mark on the recliner, just above his upper arm—"someone else's husband...someone else's wife, lingering over questions they can't answer and all that 'we could have' and 'should have' done if only...We stop fighting when we mustn't, let go of what we can change, drinking poison in large quantities and waiting for the other one to die first, taking turns pointing a finger, bleeding and hurting. We are notoriously unreliable, like hand grenades, regularly going off when disturbed. And when silence explodes, it does it with a *roar*!" (I force a deep crescendo through my open mouth like a lion.)

"Life should be happier than that," he says, trying to keep his back straight.

"Yes, like falling pregnant"—I watch him slouch back down into the comfort of his recliner—"not disgust-inducing, like when you notice chewing gum stuck underneath your shoe, which your baby boy will put in his mouth."

I grab my things, head slowly toward the door.

"That what you're running away from is impossible to run away from, you tell yourself, you crush it, along with each and every rebellion of the heart, only to bump into it when you least expect it—like your dusty earring his wife found who knows where, like his rusty wedding ring your husband found who knows when."

"Tomorrow? Same time?" he grins mechanically, adjusting his tie knot, eyes on the notes in front of him.

"Maybe...maybe not," I reply with a shrug of resignation. "There's nothing left doc, except a wilderness of disorder—and nothing else."

I close the door firmly behind me, and spill myself onto the street, flooded by colors and ridiculously alive. Clouds blot out the moon, looking run-down and neglected tonight. Dropping my head forward and pressing my chin into my chest, I think of my hands, stiff in the pockets like a starched white collar, go to the nearest bar and have two tequilas in a row.

"What's wrong?" the bartender asks, organizing the counter on the serving side.

He's got plenty of space there that enables him to move freely without tripping on things. He takes his job seriously, makes sure everything's easily reachable and displayed in an appealing way. They thought of everything, hand drying glasses too—a great investment if you want to avoid your glasses looking all smudged.

"Nothing," I say, burying my face in my arms, braid like a thick black rope around my neck—the way I'd choose to go. "Look, I'm not in the mood, no hard feelings. Maybe some other time, ok?"

"Everything is something," he turns philosophical. I do too, my little eyes peeking out, "Even total nothingness?"

He puts two cups down, fingernails like the espresso machine—elegant and clean. "Why don't we make something out of nothing?"

I raise my head the way you lift the lid on a pot of soup. "The gaps are too deep, the air too thin to fill them."

"I'm all ears," he smiles, his hands on the counter, head tilted forward, "can I get you something else to drink, Miss?"

The corners of my mouth curve up as I take a slow, steady breath, undoing the knot in my hair, let it spill over my shoulders. "I wouldn't mind a coffee...Just make it strong, please. I like my coffee strong."

Color-blind

My Thursday student hates the big clock in her apartment with white furniture and white walls. She particularly hates it when we do grammar, rolls her eyes up every five minutes wondering why time goes by so slowly. She twirls her hair talking about an Italian boy she met at a summer camp, and a German one she Skypes with under the blankets when the night falls.

My student doesn't have a favorite actor, or answer to the question *what do you want to be when you grow up?* She hates meat on her plate, warm sunny days, the beach, the beach on warm sunny days. She hates long phone calls about nothing, social outlets, noise, and skin that's cold and clammy. And school, being 14, her snobby classmates and teachers spewing out molten rocks like volcanoes—probably me too—and a bus trip with her classmates and teachers to the traffic-crammed streets of Berlin, big cities, dirty cities, drunken people, history and shopping in dirty big cities. She loves the mountain breeze, her grandparents on her mother's side, her fat cat with a funny name and two nameless guinea pigs squeaking in the cage.

My Thursday student's parents have another child no one speaks of, and a white caravan car with a GPS named Sandy that takes them to the camping world every August. On Thursdays, her mother says *Grüß Gott* and *Auf Wiedersehen, I gotta run*, mumbling something about a fabulous time she hopes her daughter had at school. When she walks out the door, she'll keep smiling from the old pictures on the kitchen tiles, face like a child's—serene, beautiful. On Thursdays, I used to see her father saying *Grüß Gott* and *Auf Wiedersehen, I gotta run*. I don't see her father anymore.

After our Thursday class, my student will watch other people's laughter on TV in the living room packed with paintings of running horses. On weekends, she'll stay in her room with colorful walls, make paper heart chains listening to pop rock songs about a place for her somewhere out there. "When I ask, I get the 'that's a stupid question' look," she said once, "so I'm like, why ask?"

The cardigan my student is wearing today reminds me of this guy who had a thing for sweaters. "What are you wearing?" he asks at 7 as he walks into the office.

"Sweater."

"Underneath?"

"Nothing."

"Meet me at lunchtime," he says from his lower throat to get a deeper voice, "don't put on a bra." (He hates touching my breasts with the bra on.)

He calls me at 8 to meet him at 12—"Are you unconsciously spreading your legs when you hear me?" At 9, he wants me to see him at 11—"Your panties getting wet, baby girl?" At 10, he tells me to meet him right away. He loves how my voice cracks every time I say *yes*. I love how he tries to keep his emotions in check every time. He grabs a few bites—says he ate enough—flips me like a pancake and fucks me on the back seat of his white truck, with the sweater on. I walk into the men's restroom afterwards to watch him pee.

"We're perfect," he says, shaking his twitching cock.

"You think so?"

"I know so. It's the world we live in that's so damn imperfect."

"Will you always love me like this?" I ask in a Nastassja Kinski kind of way.

"Like what?"

"Like the movies—till the end of the world and back."

"Always, baby. Always."

And he did—just like the movies.

My Thursday student talks about the drama at school and the shooting nearby—choppers in the sky and guns on the ground, and black spiders climbing white school walls who insisted that the bags should be opened and the contents laid out.

"Mom, it was so exciting!" she exclaims as mother changes the lipstick and shoes, flats for high heels.

"What was?"

"The shooting, mom! It was like the movies!"

"Nothing's like the movies," mother says in a loud rapid whisper, looking for approval from me.

I nod as she pulls the door shut.

"How are you doing?" I ask my student, watching her bra straps creeping out over her shoulders.

"What do you mean?" She watches me tuck mine under a sleeveless top.

"How are you feeling today?"

"Not sure I'm feeling anything."

"You tired?"

She munches on corn, like an animal brought to the slaughterhouse, unaware of a heavy blow that will stun her before neck cutting.

"Angry?"

"Nope. Sad—yes, sad," she confirms, looking away.

My student tells me about her wacko neighbor, whose wacko dog pulled loose from his hand to chase her cat across the street, and her best friend with the sun in her hair and under her skin.

"She's a real chatterbox, but I don't mind. Best friends don't have to like everything about each other. She's got a soft spot for vanilla whereas I'm more of a chocolate type. We still have a lot in common, though. When we go to the movies, we hold hands screaming together at the rear of the theater. I love her conditionally."

"Unconditionally, you mean?"

She frowns as if at a loss. I do too but she pays no mind.

" 'What's wrong?' she asks me the other day, 'you don't look so good'. I tell her it's nothing. It was easier to lie."

"Is it ok to lie to your best friend?"

"I wasn't lying. I was just economical with the truth," she quotes me, the corner of her mouth quirking up suddenly. "When I'm sad, I don't want her to know. I don't think she'd understand."

There's nothing wrong with you. There's a lot wrong with this world, I want to tell her as I button up my shirt—but I don't.

"She's so happy. She wouldn't understand," my Thursday student says, and for the first time doesn't check the clock.

A Punch in the Chest That Killed Me

Mom was mostly there, drumming her fingers on the cheekbone, blanket thrown negligently around her legs. It was as if she wasn't, though, always busy glancing across the house at some faceless danger looming out of the darkness. Couldn't shake the feeling someone was preying on us, pushing open the front door or breaking the glass in the rear one, but when I looked around, nothing was missing. She'd puff out her cheeks, voice flat and thin, as though she just realized our new toaster didn't toast a perfect bagel and was therefore disappointed, saying things like *oh, that's too bad*, as if to say *it's time we bought another one.*

And then there was him, mom's third husband (third time unlucky), my stepdad with a filthy mouth and a temper on a short fuse, face turning crimson with rage every time I'd hit the call button to the CPS. Such things only made him beat me harder. *I'll cut your tongue off if you tell anyone*, he'd snarl and kick me in the chest, then again, over and over again, until I started coughing up blood, each time thicker and stickier and harder

14

to swallow. He was larger and stronger, had those Popeye arms with heavy fists that toughen by punching. Then, one day he stopped.

It was a few months back. I was taking a nap after lunch when I woke up to him yelling at mom, so I went downstairs to see what was going on and as soon as I entered the kitchen, he gave me a death stare. Came up and roared at me, calling me names and waving his deer horn handle knife around, his breath sweltering hot on my lips.

"Look at this sturdy piece," he said and his chin moved forward, the end of his nose rising into the air. "A stunning piece of craftsmanship, manually cut and made especially for me. Impressive, don't you think? I'd been worried sick the handle would be light and not the most durable one, you know, but man was I wrong! I can see this baby lasting forever. Fits so nicely in my hand. I said, look!" he cried like a ram stabbed by its own horn, fingers wrapped tightly around the handle. "The blade may not be that sharp," he went on running it against mom's cheek, "but it carves things beautifully and will take the skin off."

I told him not to try anything stupid, and he pushed her and hit her in the face with a closed fist, knife slipping out of his hand, before he punched her square in the chest. I felt my ribs crack and break with each punch he threw at her—but stood and stared. I just stood there like a single leafless tree on top of a hill a few feet away from where lightning struck, then managed to throw some punches with my right hand after mom's cries snapped me out of it, and he fell down. Stayed down while I was throwing punch after punch after punch after...When I realized what I was doing, I took a step back, and there he was—passed out, jaw covered in blood.

I struggled for air, coughed long as if choking on a mouthful of something bitter. When I caught my breath, I asked mom if she was alright and she jerked her neck, like when your collar's too tight, making the stop gesture with her hand, so I asked no more. I pretended to be her, did what she would do—took pity on him, and let him stay. Couldn't pick him up, though—the asshole was too heavy for my thin-veined arms—so I washed his face right there and left him lying on the floor. The thought occurred to me that he only looks slimy, his skin surprisingly dry to the touch, before I went back to bed and slept for hours. When I snapped awake, my bones ached so I crawled out of bed to take a shower, then went down to check on him—but he wasn't breathing.

It's a strange feeling when you learn that the monster of a spider in the bath is actually harmless. Mom was fragile all the same, curled up beside him, one arm round his neck, fingers tangling in the black hair at his nape—stiff and still and ageless in her palms, like grass. There was something heartbreaking about him, something intelligible. He was beautiful, looked exactly as he was supposed to.

Chin against my throat, I tied my shoes quickly and headed out the door, brushing against the walls like a slow-moving shadow, body hot and airless like that afternoon. The sounds of our street trailed off into silence as I sped off.

I let my car take me wherever it wanted. Thought how easy it is to get lost.

The night was pitch-black and muggy on the outer edge of town, nearest the place where everything ends, when I finally pulled over, the ER ignoring me for hours after admitting me. I thought it was evident—broken ribs, eye the size of a tennis ball, a gaping cut in my chin—but the doctors said *it's all in your head* and *there's nothing to worry about*, so I was discharged the following day. The following day, I didn't feel any different, looked like an engraved pocket knife—handcrafted, with a heavy weight to it, perhaps smaller than expected, though the stains were as described.

That night in the hospital, the moon will make a noise like a snarl. That night I'll think of daddy's muscles, twitching and contracting against mom's bruised heart, marrow spilling out faster than resentment, or despair, think how he'll groan and moan and squeak like a pussy when they press on his chest in the morgue, tear his belly open to take a closer look. *You seem younger, daddy*, I'll say, *much younger. I haven't seen you so young.*

17

(Not that I regret it.) *Death seems to have smoothed away your wrinkles, being the ultimate Botox and all.*

That night I'll picture myself laying back in a recliner months later, unwinding after a tiring day at work by daydreaming about daddy. I'll think how I don't even know when or where she buried him (in the basement or behind the house for all I care), how I can hear him for miles, his noisy little corpse, transparent and oh so brittle, eating itself before turning into soap. Most of him will be gone soon—charcoal bones laid out like a pile of kindling—soon it'll be as if he was never there. Soon I'll think how he's slipping through my fingers all the time.

The following morning, I didn't bother to go back. I knew mom would say *go, leave me alone,* so I did. She wouldn't try to stop me anyway. In my mind's eye, there's a chair jammed up against the front door, deer horns neatly arranged around the house. *The blades with bone on stand displays came very sharp,* she'd state just as he would, *you have to watch out when opening. They hold the knives like they should, though.*

A few hours after I'd left the hospital, my muscles started to jerk, body turning colder, then deadly cold, till all I could feel was my joints stiffening—nothing more, nothing less. Within days, I couldn't bend my limbs, which left me rather numb and, with time, rigid—as rigid as a strap of metal, an inflexible knife blade. I had no logical explanation for it whatsoever, just thought it was unsettling to know he might be watching me.

At first I thought it's the recliner, that is my habit of sitting at an angle, often leaning to one side. It struck me I needed better spine support—something that wouldn't fatigue my back or damage it in the long run—so I got myself a new chair, then another one, and another one, thinking it may take a while before my body begins to relax again.

But after weeks of resisting, the walls started closing in on me. Eventually I gave in to something bigger, something much stronger. Went faster than I thought I would. (It smells like rotting teeth, like setting yourself on fire.)

Before long my body began to take on colors, the whites of my eyes drying out. Before long I was juiceless, noiseless, undramatic—scorched and bare like the slopes I grew up on. Before long I was nothing but a skeleton, cartilage, bits of dried skin—odorless and fixed in time.

Someday we'll be distant and boneless, daddy and I, the dust swelling up under our feet too thin to grow anything heavy.

Somewhere in the stillness of the night, we'll sit quietly next to each other, watch deer come closer.

I Keep Her as a Key in My Breast Pocket

When we got divorced, we divided assets. I took the toaster. She took the parasol. It happened so fast. I woke up one day to a heap of dirty laundry lying at the foot of the bed. The fridge was empty. I watched how animals hunt for food on TV.

Then I was forced out of my job. They told me it's based on my engagement level. (I think I was just too exhausted to care.) A headhunter left me a voice mail the other day but I've been in no rush to get back *at my earliest convenience*. "I wouldn't wait too long to accept the job offer," a friend said. "They'll take it off the table before you know it."

I can't think about it now. Right now my head's at buying some furniture, choosing the right coffee table and the like. She was more into aesthetics. She'd know which to pick. I could take measurements this week and go shopping sometime soon. The proper height is apparently the same height as the cushions on the sofa or 1–2 inches lower, that is two-thirds the length of the sofa or something. I'm not sure about space between the coffee table and the seating surrounding it, though. 15 inches? 30? There's so much room. I might get more stuff to fill it up, but not today. Tomorrow's another day—or not.

The thing is, there's something I need to do tomorrow. I've been having this weird feeling like there's something stuck underneath my ribcage, something that shouldn't be there, so I plan on seeing my doctor. He'll do blood work, urine labs, send me for an ultrasound and all will come back normal. After running his hand over my chest for a possible swelling or bulge, he'll give me a quick smile as if to say *as soon as we bandage up your heart, you'll be good to go.*

I'll wash my hands first thing in the morning, then pee in a cup until it's about half empty. On the way out, I'll see my next-door neighbor in the hallway. I always do, like I can always tell she's been crying. Counting the seconds between her silences and outbursts feels like counting the seconds between a flash of lightning and the strike. We confide about the necessity of smacking a child, though I don't plan on having one, and all I can think about is my ex's ass getting red from spanking.

I've never noticed it before. My neighbor's breasts look like apricots, round and full apricots which are my favorite fruit but if there's one thing I love more, it's sucking on the pits after eating them. I picture her munching her breakfast toast— all those crumbs getting trapped in the corners of her mouth—

wonder how she sighs, rolling her r's (*ay papi, yo estoy arrecho, sooo horny*), if she screams turning into *polvo*. On the Internet, girls are posting pictures of themselves with a lot of cleavage and all, hard nipples pressing against their tops. I'll jerk off before bed, curling my toes and tightening my legs and buttocks, my wife's face flickering on the walls like a neon sign. The ceiling will topple over when I try to touch her.

She loved my scruff against her cheeks. I won't shave. Might as well dispose of razor blades.

The weather forecast says rain in days and weeks to come. I'll take her as an umbrella when I go out, although it no longer rains like it used to when we were kids.

Life to the Throat

"Aknife will always manage to surprise you, like your period," I told my little girl, giving her one as a gift when she started bleeding. "That blood running prepares you for pregnancy. Learn how to use it."

I wish I'd had one. I was so confused.

You see more hair growing in new places, your body shape changing, hips and breasts getting bigger, they tell you it's nothing to worry about, it's an important part of growing up, and you're confused, having no one to talk to as everybody's busy slitting throats and maintaining edges—sex is a dirty little word anyway—you think, think some more until you stop and have your first sex, bloody sex, drunken sex, so drunk you can't recall who you had it with the morning after or any other, you just remember that morning, the burning sensation in your vagina and an empty house with naked floors, and another one crawling with people you don't know by their first names, fishing nets above and a thick carpet underneath to reduce the screams in the hallway, and a bed holding a knife that threatens to cut you open, and every other bed gaping like an open tomb, and enough tears to create a landslide till there's none left to cry, and the murder of babies you want to forget as a 13- and 14-year-old Catholic daughter—pro-life my ass—and *don't you dare tell anyone, whore!* because the world would split open and swallow everyone they call by their first name, such things aren't discussed in polite company or any other for that matter.

When you finally fall in love with someone, you find it hard to believe they love you, you of all people—battered and fractured—and why the fuck did they stop loving you then, maybe they loved you too much or they just said they did, not how you needed to be loved, you think you'll never love again and then you meet your future husband your family thinks the world of, and he meets your miscarriages and of course you can't conceive, it's a punishment from the gods above, but you lead a decent life, regardless, though you can't cum with someone you love, a whore stays a whore and should be treated as such, when her stomach howls like mating wolves, she needs to be fed a cock although she gets it at home, then there's the morning after but you don't have the pill and you're wasted all the time so you won't have to remember who got you pregnant, you hear of cinnamon powder with water and eat pineapples and sesame seeds like never before, and lie in the bathtub for hours with a coat hanger between your legs hoping god takes it, but what if you bleed to death, you'll burn in hell

and people will talk, you wouldn't do that to your husband—
maybe it's a sign.

Then everyone starts asking *how come her hair is so black?*

She's the black sheep, like mama, you joke to take the
pressure off others joking about it.

Suddenly, they stop—tongueless little birds. The
silence is so thick you can cut it with a knife.

We don't wear laces in our shoes, my baby girl and I.
We stick the tongues out from underneath our pants hanging
loosely round our hips.

(When I comb her hair, sometimes we cry.)

Nothing Like a Good Old Knife

"There's nothing worse than cutting with a dull knife," my granny would say as she cut the meat into uniform cubes. Besides, she didn't like too many gadgets in the kitchen, although she had a pretty decent collection in the attic, cupboards and old boxes under the couch, and never got used to using choppers, dicers, grinders or anything else that would cut the food mechanically.

My family has always had a thing for knives.

"I don't see how any chopper would get me pieces better than a knife would," grandpa used to say. He didn't believe in the electric knife either—"No, I don't think it'd work that well, especially with frozen meat"—and it's not like he didn't try because he did, more than he liked to admit.

Granny even had one of those old-style French fry cutter machines but was positive it wouldn't work either. Thawed meat was too soft and pliable for it, partly frozen meat stuck to the damn thing and if it was completely frozen, well, it wouldn't go through, would it? They tried it on chicken as well—for chicken strips—but it was no good, even after oiling the cutters. The blades weren't sharp enough for their liking—that's all there is to it.

I remember grandma talking about a saw they had at the farm, though apparently nothing could beat her father's razor-sharp knives when cutting the meat into picture-perfect cuts, with special attention given to steaks, which had to be perfectly equal in thickness, and roasts, which had to be perfectly trimmed.

Game meat was particularly held in high regard, and she watched her father sharpen the knives for skinning and gutting deer on a regular basis, hot blood dripping down his hands onto the ground as she wiped the flesh down with her mother to remove anything that clung to the meat. "Let her clean the neck, belly and inside of the ribcage," father would say, "this is where most hairs and dried blood collect," after which he'd finely trim the hairy parts off.

Once, when granny was little, he gave her a rather dull knife so she could try to cut the meat herself, which was, in her words, "an unforgettable way to learn to appreciate a good tool."

My great-grandfather knew deer anatomy inside out. "We start by removing the front legs from the body, cutting meat away from the bone"—he taught his only child. "Just follow the muscle lines"—grandma showed the skill to her six children. "Cut the muscle free from where it attaches to the ribs before moving to the back legs"—I still hear mother say while I help apply pressure, my two brothers pushing them downward so she'd easily cut through the joint.

Choosing the right knife is like buying a house for my parents, uncles, aunts, cousins and siblings—*an investment meant to last*, provided you make a fine choice, apart from proper maintenance, of course. Knives are inherited in my house from one generation to the next, like fears and traumas, and for the record we've had plenty of those, bleeding mothers being the most common one and the least spoken of.

My mom, for example, has never overcome a fear of thunder and lightning she inherited from her mother, who used to fold herself like a map—very neatly, along the dotted line— before she went into the closet to hide, howling and scratching from inside like a puppy. When I was little, each time a storm began, mom would sit us down in the hall with closed doors and no windows and cover us with a blanket, without letting go of our small hands, until it went away or we fell asleep on the floor. My dad, who's in his late 60s, still checks weather reports several times per day and generally avoids traveling by night, whereas I myself tend to cancel all plans at even a slight possibility of a thunderstorm.

***

I come from a long line of butchers to whom slaughtering cows, pigs, lambs, rabbits and poultry, dressing their flesh and selling their meat have become second nature, which is why the village people call us slaughterhouse dwellers or throat slitters.

"It's a business like any other," my grandfather would say, wiping his bloody hands on the apron before washing his knives and countertops with hot, soapy water. "It feeds us, pays our bills. Don't you dare be ashamed of it."

I sure as hell ain't, gramps. How could I?

Animals hanging from the shackling chain, knives being inserted through the skin and heads being detached by cutting through the neck have been a part of my life for as long as I can remember. I grew up watching liquid fire spurting out and flowing freely, death occurring seconds later, learning how to handle raw meat and cut it up with slicers and band saws from practically every member of my family. Mind you, meat needs to be perfect in color and texture to find its place in one of our many cooking pots and pans. Luckily, butchering allows you complete control over meat so, since its quality is of utmost importance to us, we breed animals at our own farm, kill them, eat them and sell them.

Everyone goes about butchering differently. I mainly kill animals by slitting their throats or by direct blow to the skull, making sure it's smashed right away. My children have become pretty skillful at it too, though the little one has never gotten used to killing chickens as much as my husband and I would want her to.

"You're not getting any younger," my grandfather told me on his deathbed, "if you wish to stay competitive and this business to last, you're gonna need some fresh blood around here."

Anyway, she tried to wring a chicken's neck a while ago but messed up.

"Use the rope!" we yelled. "That's what it's for." She wouldn't listen.

Unless you're fast when you start pulling the head off the bird, it can get pretty messy, which is precisely what happened. The chicken fell to the ground, began to blink and thrash about, then ran around spraying blood everywhere while she ran after it like a headless chicken, mouth and eyes wide open, until she stopped all of a sudden and lifted her hand up, watching blood dripping from the knife and falling onto her milk-white dress, stains getting bigger as she rubbed her fingertips against a thick heavy silk. She never wore it again. Says it looks like a bandage, red soaking through.

I felt bad for her but knew feeling bad wouldn't stop me from eating chickens, let alone killing them. When she went in, the hen wasn't moving, yet I pressed the blade against her little throat, just in case, and she stretched out her neck. With the expression of absolute madness in her eyes, she let out a shrill gargling cry one last time before everything went quiet. There was no wind and the trees were still. I thought nothing could possibly break such a complete and utter absence of sound.

She wet the bed again last night. Said she couldn't breathe, stuffed into stacks of tiny crates with other chickens, waiting to be killed. "I hear them screaming every night," she said, ground opening its big jaws to catch the crimson rain gleaming in the sky like china cats.

I went into labor with her way too early. There was no one in the house, the horizon black with an approaching storm. I gave birth in the bathtub, cutting my newborn daughter's umbilical cord with my teeth. Afraid I'd lose her, like previous two babies, I imagined breathing sunshine back into my lungs and, hugging her to my chest, waited for the storm to pass.

"We have to be patient with her," I told my husband in bed last week as I recalled my father giving me the chicken for the first time, myself not knowing how to hold her legs, sharp claws ripping my arm open as she tried to get out of my arms. "Obviously she's not ready yet."

Yesterday we let her watch the twins do it out front. On the plus side, she has good teachers, who were thrown in at the deep end themselves but got used to it in no time. They love killing chickens with their bare hands by pulling the neck, which—they learned well—causes them the minimum amount of suffering. My little one gazes gravely and intently into their faces, legs dangling from a chair on the balcony, feet and toes ripped bloody from constantly pecking at them—always at the same spots, like she's trying to pull her baby toe off. (Says it's broken anyway, it's nothing, *I feel nothing*.) She is listless and droopy, movements slow as she says, "Love animals," quoting my grandfather as though to herself, "but when you have to kill them for food, don't feel sorry for them and never do it in anger." A moment later, the door opens and she slips in.

"What was that all about?" her father asked her later in the day, and she pressed her hands to her chest, said she was feeling queasy. Then he said there's no place for squeamishness in our family, sitting her at the table where we were cleaning chickens and plucking the feathers, and she gave me a heartfelt look. "Mom," she began to sob as I told her to try—we won't force her to do anything she doesn't want to.

For a split second, I thought it might actually work. It's a nice way to connect, like cooking and eating together, but things didn't turn out how we'd hoped. Even when all the other kids played with the raw meat, dripping it into the gooey, drizzly marinade, listening to grown-up talk, my little one crinkled up her nose in disgust, and when I asked her if she was alright, she flinched at the touch of my hand, said she heard her chicken make a gasping noise. I told her it's the weight of the dirt pushing the air from her lungs, "it's normal," but she said, "no mom, I think she's saying good-bye." It was then that I knew someday she wouldn't be able to put up with the sight of meat, even when burned.

She ate lunch with her fingers so she wouldn't have to use a knife. She'll turn her balcony into a chicken haven when she gets married and moves out, let them decide for themselves. There won't be sharp edges in her house.

***

Me, I can't get enough of wishing to own more knives, having a special connection with each and every one I've ever bought—curved and flexible ones, rigid, extra wide, extra thin, you name it—as long as the blade edge doesn't allow food to stick. Hands down, nothing thrills me half as much as holding a knife in my hand.

The knife set on my kitchen counter reminds me of all the men I've loved before, most of whom used stiff blades due to the enhanced precision in the cut—a beautiful liar who loved my neck and wrote me insane letters by flashlight, then stabbed me in the back where the neck meets the shoulders, letting me bleed out, a firefighter who failed to put out the fire, a paramedic who didn't know how to dress a profusely bleeding wound, someone busy building stairways, walls, and backyard sanctuaries, chewing gum to mask the cheap scent of hotel rooms on his breath, a guy who unclogs sinks and clogs highways, and another fella with a soft spot for multi-purpose blades—ideal for chopping hope, dicing love and slicing trust.

Knives have never been a mere cutting tool for me. I carry at least one with me at all times, as a tool rather than a weapon, jack knife being pretty convenient for opening and screwing things. Then again, I consider myself a decent knife fighter and, even though I don't go around pissing people off, I wouldn't refrain from using one to defend myself in a life-or-death scenario.

I like to think fate besides an affinity for knives brought hub and me together, because he has an envious collection himself, having a Swiss army knife on his key chain wherever he goes. Last time we whispered sweet nothings to each other, he held my hands behind my back, then pulled his knife to run the cold steel along both sides of the backbone. The feel of it against the skin, the weight of it...like love making in uppercase letters—un-fucking-paralleled.

He's got a thing for cut-throat razors as well. He'll tell you they cut sharper than modern ones, which he considers useless.

"Traditional ones are like women," he said shaving this morning, "a work of art, and if routinely cared for, they'll in turn take best care of you."

We often sharpen our knives together, but while I generally do it the old way—with a coffee mug—hub is more professional in that regard, using a whetstone or an electric knife sharpener whose staccato rhythm keeps them super sharp. I love to watch him do it, pressed against him, as he's meticulous at picking the right angle—normally a steeper, more durable one—knows exactly what angle is appropriate for which blade, sharpening one side of the knife with a single stroke before flipping it to sharpen the other one.

He woke up early today since polishing the edge takes time. I shot out of bed when I realized what he was doing. While gently applying pressure in a circular motion with both hands, I rolled my waist forwards and back slowly, feeling prickles in my arms and at the back of my legs, like when you're lying on the stiff dry grass.

"When the time comes"—hopefully not before—"I'd like to die from a knife...or at least with one," I said resting my head on his shoulder. The veins in his neck started throbbing.

I cut my index finger with a knife recently, watched a dark, maroon shade of red gush out like piping-hot water. Outside the window, it was a night of wind and rain. I couldn't move. It felt like I'd fallen into a crack somewhere.

"Let me have a look," hub said leaning over, movements firm and precise, his bulk overshadowing both of us.

He appeared calm. I thought he was more composed than I'd ever been.

"There's nothing worse than a blunt knife," he lowered his voice to a whisper. "I'll make sure I sharpen it today."

Smile for Me, Baby

Lyv, my name is Lyv, and I rarely smile. This is me at the age of 16 smiling, because it's a modeling picture—you have to smile when you're modeling. I didn't think much in this picture. I had just signed with a top agency in New York City. I saw only stars. There's no time to think when there's places to be and runways to walk.

"The size will be 00, you'll have to be able to fit into it by September," I was told, so I fasted down to 90 pounds. The agency loved it. Agencies love their girls' waif-like figures, wrists and fingers getting too small for the jewelry they once wore.

In some of these pictures, I look small and insignificant. Here, for example, I'm out of focus whereas the background is sharp, as if I was slowly fading behind the labels. Figured I'd get past it—as long as I bear in mind calories are my enemy. Nothing looks good on you when you're fat. Mother too says super thin girls appear more glamorous on the catwalk while she chuckles in rooms that crawl with agents sticking their hands up our skirts, and photographers with white noses who call us *baby*.

In this one, I'm the spitting image of the umbrella I'm carrying. We were almost swept away by a strong wind. I tried to save it by stepping on it, and when I stepped on it, it went up and when it went up, I thought it would never fall back down, and when it finally did, I watched it fall down with a thud.

At this point in this picture I wanted to disappear, covering myself up like a mummy so people would stop staring at my dangling joints and collar bones jutting out, afraid they might notice I no longer had my period. The industry didn't mind, though. The industry teaches you to be confident by stopping you from being comfortable with curves and seeing women of different sizes as pretty.

Other girls use feet and tusks to dig waterholes for drinking and bathing, which is about the only thing they are willing to share. Our father stands at the bathroom door, poised with his sword raised, mother obsessively subscribing to online magazines about cooking and watching health documentaries on Netflix. And we breathe on our fingers, lowering ourselves into the chair, say *it's freezing in here*, again, *can't I turn on the heating*, bundled up in coats and scarves even in the hottest weather.

Stop it, you cry baby! I'd scream and slap myself in front of the mirror. You can't handle a little pressure? Fine! Then go back to your little town with little people in it who can't wait to see you fail, binge eating when they don't feel good about themselves. Being thin and famous is everything you ever dreamed of. Suck it up! If you flop this time, you'll never get to see the world's fashion capital—it'll be all *your* fault.

So I'd stay, feeling as if I'd overeaten again, nibbling on food before the cameras, then racing to the bathroom to bend over the basin. I used to go days without feeding my dog when I noticed he unnecessarily put on weight. Poor bastard!

This is me at 17, minutes before I turn deathly white and faint backstage. I thought it was a phase. I thought I had a choice. Doctors feed me through a tube that goes from the nose to the stomach, suggest I keep a food journal. (Monday through Saturday: three apples a day and as much diet coke as I wish. Sunday: a piece of fish/ chicken.)

This one's kind of funny. I look wild, watering the plants on my balcony, encouraged by the unseasonably warm evening and windows held wide open. It was taken when I stepped on the hose and choked it up. I'm smiling, happy that color has returned to my face. Smiling, not knowing I won't live to see the day I turn 18.

Veg Garden for Beginners

"The rains have started early this year," mother said, tucking in sheets on both sides of the couch, scarf knotted tightly under her chin, as I entered the kitchen with a loaf of bread, still warm against my chest—"my hydrangeas and bleeding hearts will love it." A faint smile crept across her face, like a candle that flickers a couple of times before going out. "Did you get wet?"

I thought of my brother and me waiting with our tongues out for the first drops to fall, and my boys who prefer bouncing on beds. "No," I murmured, "it's just a light drizzle."

She smoothed everything down, getting the kitchen all straightened up before the kids came down, then lifted her shoulders in a little shrug, her voice abruptly serious. Said she hadn't shaven her man in days, said it was unthinkable, said keeping the whiskers off his face would make him feel more comfortable, "what was I thinking" and "I can't wrap my head around it."

"Mom, stop!" I shouted—"it's not your fault." Then she said no one raises their voices in her family and no one fights, "don't you raise your voice at me—I am your mother!" There was a brief silence, like distant gunfire, between us before she blinked her eyes several times, as if searching for brand new words to apologize to a grown child.

Without saying a word, I pulled down the shaving kit from the top shelf above the sink. Knew she'd want to check the razor first to make sure the blade was clean and sharp. Knew it would lift the burden off her shoulders. She's got years of practice under her belt, knows exactly what's sharp enough and what isn't. "After all, the best way to tell is to shave with it," she'd say.

Mother swallowed hard and, pulling up a straight-backed chair with no arm rests, sat down, nodded yes. Legs wide apart, she took the razor out of the box, touching her damp thumb pad against the edge. Slowly, thoughtfully, like someone who doesn't want to be hurried into making a bad decision.

"It should feel sticky," she said after a pause, then looked out the window. A fine rain was coming down, pattering on the windowsill and rooftops. "It's good. He'll feel fresh after it, I know he will—newly born."

I glanced at her hands. Thought it might not be a great shave in terms of closeness but I'm sure there won't be any razor burns or bumps—father will be pleased.

Once the blade was on the table, mother made certain everything else was ready, item for item—shaving cream (check), brush (check), clean washcloth (check), basin with warm water (check), mirror (check). Wearing gloves didn't feel right so she never used them. She needed to feel the real thing, apart from frowning on anything disposable. Who could blame her? Father's face was like a pebble smoothened by the waves—no cuts, no sores—you could shave such a man every day.

She used to help him to a sitting position early on, which was undoubtedly easier for both, but that was no longer possible. The head of the bed couldn't be raised either so she leaned forward, taking her time, and, grabbing hold of the edge of the table, got to her feet again. She wet his hair a little, combing it back in an attempt to make the most of what was left of it, then tucked the towel under his chin, hand rubbing gently over his beard area. The rain became heavier. I thought of my bicycle left out front, thought of thick black clouds massing in the sky as she ensured father's face was well softened up before she started. He liked it, you could tell. Stretching the skin, she began making firm strokes, all the while shifting weight from one leg to the other, blade bouncing on his face from the sideburns down toward the chin and across the cheeks. Father quieted his breathing as though not to disturb her, slightly open mouth exposing yellowed teeth.

I checked the time—"Well, I gotta get going"—rose from the table, with the assistance of a little cane, and took the jacket off the hook, quickly going through the pockets in order not to take with me something that would for sure be taken away.

Mother held out her hand as if to touch the steadily falling rain. "It should ease off any minute, don't worry," she said. I froze like a frost-bitten plant that hates sitting in cold soil.

"Of course it will," I uttered unconvincingly after a moment's hesitation, grabbing my backpack from underneath the table.

"You should've stayed for lunch," she continued, without raising her head, "we're having cabbage. I doubt they make cabbage over there...Or they do. Some prison yards have a nice vegetable patch, with potatoes and beans and zucchini. Radishes even. I don't see why they wouldn't. You dig up a small area, remove stones and weeds."

Father sighed sharply, knew mother's choice of words wasn't a very happy one. Me, I pretended to agree with her just to keep her satisfied. I put on my jacket as fast as I could, needed to get out of there as fast as I could. I looked silly—I know I did—like a 5th grader who wants to apologize for the tics but doesn't know how.

Mother gave a distant nod, "Yes, weeds can be tricky, you need to keep those under control. Then again, it's not something you can't learn." She stopped to throw a glance at the blade—it's clogged with hair. She rinsed the razor off with warm water right away, swished it in the basin after each stroke now. "Other than that, it's no big deal, really," she went on, "you just fill the beds with compost, bury your seeds and rake the soil flat. The wait is a drag, though," her voice dropped to a hoarse whisper, "there will be plenty of time to think."

My mouth was round as if to form words, words that wouldn't come out, words they'd never get to hear. Father's face got curve shaped, small eyes brimming with a determination to hang in there as long as he could. The disease might have left him with an unusable body, but the muscles that control smiling remained intact. Mother turned his head so as not to miss a spot.

***

Our farm is only a few minutes' walk from the bus stop, from where the bus leaves for the city every two hours. When I set off, the rain had somewhat subsided so I didn't struggle to walk against it as I thought I would. By the time the deputy sheriff and I reached the Reception Center, it was pelting down again.

Inside, I take off my glasses and tuck them in my pants pocket, leave my hand there. A moment later, I see an officer walking purposefully along the hall, gaze fixed straight ahead, like someone who's at peace with his surroundings. He nods toward us, fat finger pointing to a plastic container.

Right after he's ticked the box on his form, he grabs a cup filled to the brim with coffee and shows me into a room behind the counter. It's formal and impersonal, resembles a business letter. The colors sure as hell don't look any different in different lights here.

"I'm also gonna need your ID," the officer proceeds in a stern voice, "your cell phone and, um, yeah, about the phone—you're allowed one telephone call within the first week and every month thereafter. No visitation is allowed for the first thirty days in R&C." He'll show me the mail room later, as well as the phone for placing collect calls.

Like an actor who has learned his lines by heart, he tells me about the wake-up, roll-calls, meal time, the time prescribed for walks, library books I can use all I want, then pauses to flick a fly off his hairy arm that buzzes past like a small plane. My hand feels unsteady signing the paper.

"Ok," he breathes out deeply as if relieved to have gotten at least some of his worries off his chest—the wings flutter against the window pane a few seconds before flying up in the air—"basically, you're stuck with us for a month or two; that's how long the intake process normally takes, Mr., um"—he checks my ID again to avoid making a mistake—"Smith, right? You'll be tested and evaluated in our facility before being transferred to a permanent one, but I'm sure you already know that."

He throws words with such precision he could pin that fly to a wall.

When he lifts his head, he gives me the Rhett Butler smile with a raised brow. "You may rest assured we'll find you the most suitable one," he says, handing me a big plastic bag for my clothes.

Standing naked on the marble floor, I listen to the rain beating down, my throat dry, breathing shallow and ragged, think of the right way to get oxygen back into my lungs, think it's possible to grow vegetables here. There's probably too much clay, though. How do you get the soil right when there's so much clay?

"These are your new clothes," the officer goes on, giving me my glasses back. I can also keep the photos.

As soon as I get dressed, he takes the bag out of my hand and zips it shut. My cane too, says I won't be needing it.

"When can I see my lawyer?" I ask, and he starts yelling he's the one who asks questions here, "capisce?"

"Everything but capisce."

I feel his breath in my mouth, the sucking of air into my lungs. Little rescue breaths when the chest begins to fall.

"Don't fuck with me, mister. This ain't the place."

My blood can flow again.

"And don'tchu ever, and I mean ever, talk before being asked. Did I make myself clear?"

He grabs me by the chin, thumb digging in against my cheek. "What did you say?"

"Gotcha."

"Yes, Sir!"

"Yes, Sir."

"You can receive visits from qualified clergy right away," he snickers. "I reckon you wanna pray, boy."

Within half an hour, I was photographed, fingerprinted and palm printed. Given soap, toothpaste, deodorant. Assigned a prisoner ID number, told I'd be educated on prohibited sexual conduct and how to report sexual conduct or threats. "You'll have a prisoner file created, including the investigation report, sentence and pending charges. Now do you or do you not have any questions?" he demands, as if asking for an urgent investigation into the murder.

I picture mother's red cabbage on the chopping board, hands removing loose leaves before shredding it finely and bringing their little hearts to a boil. All the magic tricks those hands can do to stop the color running.

"Suit yourself. Joe!" he calls out, wiping his nose with his hand. "Take him to his room."

Looking like he started some shit at the bar last night, Joe slaps a set of handcuffs on my wrists and guides me through the corridors, our footfalls against the bare floor sending out hollow echoes. I listen to every rattle and creak along the way—hear the distant tinkle of cow-bells, boys clattering up and down the stairs, father's teeth clinking against the rim. Mother feeds him bread and warm milk while he goes on shrinking. He'll need a small coffin, I'm sure he will, the one made for a child.

There are so many corridors to walk down, and I keep thinking Joe will open his mouth to show me his sharp tongue, jaw ready to bite, gobble me up—but no, Joe's not like that. "This is it," the ugly face says at last, voice toned down, almost hushed, before uncuffing me. I feel shivery when the music stops. I could never live somewhere where it's always cold. I wouldn't survive.

The room is of modest size—stone walls on three sides and a solid door with a small window on the fourth, two bunks, a sink and a toilet glued together. My teeth chatter as the door clicks shut. I flop onto my back—the tray's hard, the ceiling low. I rise, like a wave, then fall. Tell myself to tackle one bit at a time—don't dig up the whole garden only to realize you've taken on too much. I pull myself off the floor, slam my head against a wall.

Joe peers in through the window with a tic in his left cheek that makes him look as if he's smiling. It's not a smile, though. It's the damn tic he's gotta do, like I had to do what I did. We get this feeling in the place where the tic is, my friend Joe and I, know the only way to make it go away is to do the tic.

When Joe leaves, the clock will start ticking the minutes.

His Nightstand, Hers

After dropping out of school, you'll move to a big city and live in a studio apartment the size of a camping tent, in a walk-up crawling with cockroaches and mice. When you buy your first nightstand, you'll force it up five flights by strong will alone. (You'll decide to forever hate the broker who has promised you'll get used to the stairs.) On flight two, you'll think god is punishing you for all the wrong you've done to (not so) loved ones, wonder why everyone but you has someone who loves them enough for physical labor. By flight four, you'll regret not marrying your high school darling. After you recover, you'll say that neither an hour and a half by subway to two of the three jobs you'll be working nor your out-of-state friends bitching about your bathroom's lack of ventilation will make you stop calling this tiny, isolated island home.

The next apartment you'll share with a roommate—a straight-A student who'll realize nothing good ever happens in the front of the school bus. The two-bedroom joint will be in a bearable location, and you'll enjoy filling it with decor your stepmom will think tasteful enough.

When you move in with a guy, the walls will need to be painted, excessive pieces of furniture ditched, but the apartment will have accomplishment written all over it when done so you'll have no time to lose. Your dad will scoff at soppy love scenes. (You'll scoff at his scoffing.)

After the wedding, he'll remark casually he's pleased your husband has found you a *real* apartment in a *real* building.

From then on, you'll be working your asses off until you're ready to buy your first house. The neighbors will pitch in, help organize the housewarming party. (The massive rectangle dead center in your living room will raise a few eyebrows.)

The second house you'll want to own will make your dream of moving to suburbia come true. By dinnertime, you'll expand your vocabulary with new compound nouns such as fresh air, natural scenery and community bond. This will be the house where you'll start reproducing. Once everyone is seated, you'll announce you're knocked up for the third time.

The house you'll live in last will have ceilings the color of ashes after a fire. This will be the house where you'll die. Your husband will let you decorate it but will be clear about one thing—he will *not* want his spaces to be too girly. The only thing you'll want is a nice flow. (And continuity that comes from keeping your mouth shut for over two decades now.)

You'll call simplicity the ultimate sophistication, though there will be things you won't be able to do without, like a full fridge and medicine cabinet, as well as objects of value and functionality on your nightstand. (He'll call it clutter. You'll call it a necessity.) These will include items you'll wish to keep close when you call it a night— a dish for the stuff you'll remember to take off when already in bed, namely your wedding ring and watch, a lamp to lighten things up, a framed photo of the past and a couple of animals at your bedside (a porcelain dog and a brass horse.)

"Seeing your nightstand," he'll repeat time and time again, "feels like falling into an unmade bed," which, quite a few will note, no one's ever died from.

On a still and sultry day, you'll remake your queen-size bed after he's done it because you'll notice wrinkles in the spread. He'll say you need one size smaller. (You'll long for one size larger.)

He loves to put everything away, and will need extra storage for his underwear and remote controls for the TV, so he'll eventually buy that ugly bedside cabinet. (Seeing it feels like falling down, like falling—you'll never tell him.)

For the time being, he likes his nightstand empty, which has become obvious after his one-night stand.

"I'd always feared *it* might happen to us," you confide to your friend Julie, watching the smoke spilling in front of the fireplace, fire dying out. He insists on calling it that way because *it* doesn't mean anything. *It* is impersonal. *It* isn't any specific woman. *It* could be a man for all I care, though he's not into men, at least not that I know of, then again I've never really taken pride in attention to detail. *It* is when he's like *we're in this together* and I'm like *stay right the fuck where you are. It* sounds less guilty—that's all there is to *it*.

I have my good days and my bad days. During the good ones, I'm like a knife all blade, trying to grab hold of myself without bleeding too much, mostly keeping busy around the house so as not to be reminded of his insistence on minimalism. (Minimalism is when all you really want is only what you really need.) Truth is, I'm a mess most of the time, pissed at the whole goddam world—at myself, at him, the kids, pissed at my neighbor for digging up the tree my deep-shade plants adored, the swimming pool for overflowing, the butcher for giving me bones for free, his hairdresser for making him look so orderly. It's hard to pin down his age, let alone anything else, by looking at his face. (You're able to write a book by looking at mine.)

Mom used to say, "I'd rather die than have to watch my only child confront my mortality." She didn't trust the body, feared the ways it could turn on her. I too feel anxious when I think about how mine's going to change, with or without my consent. Deep down, she knew she'd die young. Deep down, I know I'll live long.

Julie will say, "There's no such a thing as a one-night stand." (You'll hate her like that broker. Like hell you get used to the stairs. You never get used to the stairs.)

He'll say, "I was weak. Now that the fog is gone, I see it for what it really was—dirty and shameful."

It will flash though my brain that I might actually feel better if we call it a draw. I could really do it—take evening classes or hire a good-looking hunk of a Spanish guy in his 30s to remind me of all the stuff I've forgotten—in his bed, in ours, hands on his nightstand (or bedside cabinet.)

When she finally starts touching again, it will be to women, although she's not really into women. Somehow she'll find it less disgusting.

Onion Skins

I balance a couple of bowls and plates on my wrist, think they are not stacked correctly, think carrying a tray through a crowded room—making it snappy and making them happy—is something I could never do when my neighbor friend Eva catches me off guard, staggering to the balcony with me. "You know my mom and brother died in a car accident, don't you?" she asks.

Seconds passed before I realized I had forgotten. It crossed my mind that I betrayed her—it was the closest I've ever come to feeling like a dork—but tried not to make it worse than it already was by lying as convincingly as possible.

"I do," I duck my head, hoping I look inconspicuous. Then raise my voice, unnaturally excited, to say "I'm making *gulyás* for dinner," asking her to help me peel and chop up the onions, and she forces a smile. I take it as a yes, point my crooked finger at the knife on a plate.

"They were buried in *Česká*," Eva says, moving a chair, which makes a scraping sound, then sits closer to the wall. "I was little, days into starting school, a year before I came to Hungary with my foster parents. I remember a weird feeling like something bad happened and my friends pulling my leg, calling me clairvoyant."

As if she was unexpectedly turned into a fish, Eva pauses, unsure what to do with the gills. For a moment I think about my late husband's parents who I took care of for the last two years of their life. I loved them dearly. When they passed, I would often drive to the cemetery to just sit there, thinking, remembering, looking around. Some graves were well preserved—you could tell they were tended to regularly—others crumbled to dust a long time ago.

My son István and I moved to a nearby town last year, so now I only visit the graves whenever I'm in the area. Some cemeteries, like the one where my parents and grandparents were buried, are easier to visit than others. Sadly, my husband is a bit farther off now. On the plus side, however, he and his parents are next to each other so I can visit them in one go.

Eva sits on the edge of her seat, clearly nervous, as if trying to say something, not knowing how to start. She remains indecisive for a little while as I fiddle with the onions, sorting them by color and flavor, but when she jars the silence, it feels like a lone wolf howling in the middle of winter.

"My brother died in my mum's tummy, dad tells me. She's in the hospital, giving birth to a baby who won't cry or scream or grow up with me, who'll be buried in the same grave with my mom, in the same cemetery as my dad and my nan several months later. They said the service was beautiful, 'it's good that she handled it so well,' and I was just playing hide-and-seek outside the church and they never came looking for me—hiding for hours from no one."

Blood begins to run into the corner of her eyes. She blinks as though to clear her vision. She hasn't visited their graves in over 40 years, doesn't plan on going back there. Taking an onion out of the bowl, Eva asks me about my brother. Says I haven't told her what really happened.

"True," I say. "He drowned, they never found him. I like to think the bottom of the river as his grave, which is why I go there sometimes, walk the long way from the parking lot to the water's edge to get just as close to him as I possibly can."

"At times," Eva says with the knife in her hand, "I think that's the most difficult part of growing old."

"Growing up, you mean?"

I cut the top off the red onion, bury it in a flowerpot on the windowsill. Slitting the first layer, Eva removes the skin of the brown one. She throws a glance at mine being put on the chopping board while cutting hers down the center so she can easily grab the top layer.

"No, I meant what I said—growing old. Oddly enough, it hurts more now than it used to when I was little. Despite the flares, all the aches and pains in the body," she says, peeling the onion right off of each half, "it's the sharpened edge of the scalpel of grief that cuts the deepest, hurts the worst, leaving scars that are impossible to hide."

I turn both halves down, have trouble keeping those tears away.

"You were serious about not wanting to visit the graves ever again, weren't you?" I ask, squinting in pain, looking away to give my eyes a break.

"What for?" she says. "The only thing in those boxes under the earth is empty vessels. They are not there."

"God, you sound like my son! For him it's just a place where their names are engraved."

"István's right. They live in so many amazing ways, their loss weaved through the whole fabric of our lives, into everything we've become, everything we know, it seems dishonorable to go talk to a corpse trapped in that dirt, call it my brother, my husband, my mother."

Rubbing our eyes, we conclude it's a personal thing before I tell her about a cemetery in the area where I work—very old, very unique—where I love going on a lunch break.

"Aren't you weird!" Eva exclaims.

I purse my mouth in a self-satisfied smirk. "Beautiful too—can teach you stuff. And trust me, *this* particular one is unlike anything you've seen before."

"I bet," Eva teases—but I don't care. For me it's perfectly normal to walk around a graveyard, whether you know someone who was buried there or not.

"Anyhow," I sound determined, "I recently noticed a little grave with a carving of an angel on top of the tombstone."

Eva looks like a disinterested kid, pulling at her blonde curls, legs waggling in the air. She lifts her eyebrows together as if to say *tacky*, but I insist and she listens.

"It's a simple upright slab, completely out of place amid large markers of older graves, belongs to a little girl who was only five when she died in 1972."

"Jesus!" Eva cries, surprised all of a sudden, holding her wrist as if trying to find a pulse, "it would have made her almost the same age as us."

"Exactly! I also noticed that quite often there are flowers on her grave. If her parents are still alive and in the area, they must be very old. Maybe it's her mother who never accepted her little girl's death, maybe a sibling, but someone remembers this girl who died decades ago."

I soak the onions in a bowl of cold water, then sit back to gaze at the moon—her face drawn and exhausted, beads of sweat on the forehead, dark shadows beneath her eyes— imagine this woman traveling all those miles just to kneel before her daughter's grave, just to tell her how much she loves her, how much she misses her. And then go back home and try to get some sleep—every now and then, she succeeds.

Tears streamed down Eva's cheeks. In a split second she was soaked, as though I'd squirted a water gun in her face.

"Eva? Are you—"

"I'm alright," she said—her mouth twitched some, then she smiled—"it's the damn onions."

***

"Look, there's something I need to tell you."

"What is it?" Hanna asks.

"It's my dad."

"What about him?"

"Well, when he got sick," István says, "I'd check in on him dozens of times per day, not counting the regular care or the times he called me to his room. It's been years now and yet"—he stops as if to get a rock out of his shoe—"well, I still find myself looking in to check on him, see if needs me...Am I going crazy or what?"

"It'll stop, sooner or later," Hanna says. "It has to. Don't worry. I did the same when my mom passed away. With me it lasted a couple of years, though the frequency tapered off well before then."

Hanna creases her brows, unsure whether or not to ask him about something he's been so reluctant to share. She grits her teeth, hopes for the best.

"You rarely talk about him. You said once you never visit the graves."

"Because they don't live in a hole in the ground," István says, taking out the chopping board, knives and vegetables, laying everything on the kitchen table. "Will you help me with these?" He needs to peel the rest of the onions, add tomatoes to the meat.

Hanna tosses her sweater in the corner and grabs the over-the-neck apron, puts it on, folding it once at the waist to make it a bit shorter. He helps her tie it tightly in the back, then kisses the cook—just as it says in the front.

"That's one sassy apron," István says as Hanna, a talent for quick decisive action, takes an onion and a knife to cut the sprout end off. "So tell me, smartass," she insists, "where do the dead live?"

"They don't," István frowns, "that's the thing. Mom doesn't get it either."

Hanna gives a little chuckle, calls him a self-righteous prig—it wouldn't hurt if he came along every once in a while, "It would mean a lot to her."

"I've told you a thousand times—I can't!"

"Why not?"

"Because I just can't," he confirms in a firm voice, determined to persevere, knowing she's like a kid, though. She'll keep asking questions till she gets the answers she thinks she deserves. "Can we please drop it?"

"I don't think so," Hanna says playfully, then begins to throw tomatoes and onions in the air, catches them quickly, keeps them moving. "István, look," she shines, "you've always wanted to learn how to juggle—it's easy, look!" When she puts the veggies down, she suggests he should start off by tossing scarves instead of balls. "Fire comes in the end."

"You like the heavy stuff, don't you—cemeteries, and all? What's with the obsession?"

"I'd rather call it a fascination," Hanna says, sitting down. "Whenever I'm in a new town, I often drive through the local cemetery."

"You crazy."

"They can be interesting places. I read once that some languages were found to be carved on gravestones long after the language stopped being spoken in some communities. Amazing, isn't it?"

"Very," István grimaces and huffs as Hanna goes on.

She loves the rural ones, with a local history and moss-covered monuments—"All those axes and rakes make you think."

"Fucking hell! You're crazier than my mom."

"Which is why you love me."

István shrugs his shoulders helplessly, places the knife on the root and slices the onion vertically. When Hanna tells him about a poignant headstone she came across last year, his heart grows heavy. He trusts his instincts, clenches his chest.

"It wasn't old. Don't know, maybe five years old, could be ten. There are three etched portraits of a father and his two boys, aged three and seven—most likely a car crash."

He glances at the time. Barely a few minutes have passed and he's tired already. He's not exactly a culinary artiste, proposes ordering pizza, but Hanna wants something home-made so she takes a sharper knife to chop the onions, running her finger along the blade before she gets down to work.

"How do you know?" He makes a half-hearted attempt to sound friendly, watching the onions being stabbed to death.

"Well, the father and older son's date of death are the same whereas the younger son's is one day later, which means—"

"That two died right away while the little one died the following day from injuries."

"Bingo!"

"Now check this out. The inscription on the gravestone said something like '*in immortality we are free*'." István ponders that for a moment, decides he doesn't like the taste of it, and she goes on to say there weren't flowers on the grave, as if they'd never received a single visitor. "Makes you wonder what happened to the woman because if she had died, she would have been buried next to them, right?"

A slow silver moon has risen in the sky. István stands by the table, glaring at it accusingly through the glass door. Why can't it stay full and round? he wonders. Before long it will get smaller, until there's no moon at all and everything turns completely dark.

The silence grows heavier. Hanna feels as if she sent him five texts in a row without a reply in between. Brushing the hair out of her face, she asks what he'll do when she dies, if he'll come visit her.

"I won't need to," István says wryly. "I'll have you cremated—ashes scattered, job done." Tells her not to worry, though, he'll keep her remains close ·by, like one of those ancient widowers, feeling close to their wives of more than sixty years.

"Give me that. I'm a pro at dicing onions!" Hanna cuts in, seeing István has stopped cutting, although his issue is actually peeling them. The skin is tough to get off. He's never sure just how many layers to peel off.

"What if I die first?" he asks, eyes on his skin, suddenly dry as beef jerky.

"Nothing," Hanna says calmly, "I'll bring you flowers."

She holds the onion face down on the chopping board, knife flat against her hand, and the tips of his fingers arch.

Helium

Perhaps my doctor's right. Perhaps it's time to let go.

My husband says he's starting to feel like a machine, says *I'm afraid you only need me for my sperm*, says *maybe we shouldn't, I'm afraid*, he says, *I'm so afraid*. He wants us to sit and talk—so not sexy!

Yeah...it's clear by now I'm not the most fertile woman in the world. Let's put it this way—getting me pregnant is virtually impossible. It's so impossible they need to make up a new word for *impossible*. Even when I conceive, my pregnancies don't last. No medical explanation has ever been given—seems I'm just unlucky.

Perhaps hub's right. Making a baby has become a science experiment. It was hard enough the first time. For years I had been religiously noting down how I was feeling and where I was feeling it. Every time I'd change something, be it a diet or a regime of rest and meditation, I'd fill out a spreadsheet, having a feeling it would work *this* time, though even saying it felt like I was tempting fate. "Fingers crossed,"

I'd tell hubby. He'd heave a sigh, press the temple with his upper palm.

For years I'd rubbed my little statues, waited for a full moon to rise over the valley, for years I avoided sweeping under the bed, paid no attention when he said *it's a lousy excuse not to vacuum*. He said not to buy into that new-agey crap when I got myself a rose-quartz bracelet. Said it's all hocus-pocus, *I can't believe you fell for it again*, when I suggested we should change sexual positions more often. (With us, it's mostly a grateful girl on her back and a nice guy pumping away in missionary position for three minutes before collapsing. Feels like getting blood drawn—let's just get in there and get it over with.) He said it after our second round, though, looking all dog-tired, his tail hanging kind of low.

"What are we going to do now?" I asked.

"Don't know about you," he said," but I'm calling it a night—gotta get up early in the morning." I wondered if he was still into babies, wondered if it was too late to wake up with a smile.

Friends used to say time is all it takes, that no amount of supplements, dietary alterations and bed acrobatics make a difference. As for me, well, I thought everything's worth a shot when you're desperate. Old wives' tales gave me the illusion of control, which was all I needed especially when the pandemic hit, and it hit hard. Hub said we needed discipline, needed to do the same things in the same order every day for the sake of safety and the much-needed peace of mind such actions were likely to bring. It was a pretty daunting prospect, having to settle into lockdown routines. I felt like a submariner. I was supposed to train myself to come to terms with isolation while trying not to scream.

For years I'd been hysterical with grief and frustration, for months just plain numb. And lonely. Everyone knew how badly I wanted it, and yet most were afraid to ask if we were *still* trying. Not to upset me, I guess, which sort of did. Me, I never felt able to throw it into conversation, regardless of how I was feeling, so I'd slip words under my tongue, pretend nobody's home.

It was different with hubby because, sooner or later, we'd pick up where we'd left off. He only needed to glance in my direction for me to find myself in the family mood again. Besides, every single month that went by some new symptom appeared, like my boobs would tingle like nothing before, and I'd phone him at work to tell him I was absolutely positive *this* time. Every single month that went by convinced me *this* is the month, only for my hopes to come crashing down over and over with the arrival of my period.

At some point, I was knackered, said, "What do you think we blow all our baby savings on travel?" And then—

bam! I got my line on the stick, which looked so unreal that I for one thought I was imagining it.

"It's a miracle," hub said. But to me it seemed faint, somehow too short, too narrow, dunno, as if the test was asking ME *are you for real?* As if it expected me to say *of course not, I was just kidding.* I'll be lucky if the line's still there when I get back, I thought putting the kettle on, which was my way of saying *I'll give you some time to change your mind. Whatever the outcome, I need you to be 100 % sure.* Then after a while, it got fuller, longer, like a big fat bone protruding through your leg—too conspicuous to go unnoticed. My pulse raced. I could feel it in my throat. Ten long years of crying over the stick I'd peed on and one of the little fuckers finally did the job.

I'd never felt so beautiful. It was like falling in love again, like walking the streets in my red coat for nine months. I wanted people to see me, wanted them to see me in my red coat.

Perhaps I should really focus on the hand I have. I got four aces after all. (A daughter counts triple.) Perhaps it's not in Mother Nature's cards for me to have another baby.

It's just that I've always imagined two children—a girl and a boy. Clearly it's hard to accept that it ain't gonna happen for me. Like it's hard to meet my friends' new babies, when I so desperately want to be happy for them—when I crumble inside. The hardest part, though, has been watching my sisters shop for loose clothing and fill themselves with water, listening to how heavy their bodies feel as they waddle across the house, how ugly when saliva escapes from their mouths, how neither of them wanted this in the first place *and look at us now.* I've heard it before—*it just happened.* It's so not fair.

Just watching them makes me nauseous, I'm bloated and achy and itchy. Their breasts are growing, skin stretching, I hear their babies' hearts going boom boom boom, feel them squirming and fidgeting—I rub and stroke my bump.

They said we might always consider alternatives, but it seems pointless to be even thinking about surrogacy or adoption when we're all of a sudden so distant. They said I should join a local pregnancy-loss support group. And say what? That it hurts to see such abundant fertility around, to watch their days getting shorter, nights longer, future worth living for—that it hurts like hell. I could make something up, a new job offer or something, then come back when they are flat again. I find it hard to be around them. I don't love them. I'll love them later. This is not a good time for love.

Today is lunch at mom's. I see it already. Everyone will be there. Mama hens too. They'll compliment me on my figure, they'll want to talk, to share, they'll show me their babies' last pictures, flapping around and cackling, they'll purr to their eggs, little chicks peeping back to them from inside the eggs. They'll reminisce about the past when all doors stayed locked, all the silly things we used to do. *What a time to be alive*, they'll say. *We got through it together*, they'll repeat, *together, together.* They'll think back to when the three inseparable piglets dropped a stone down their grandpa's well. Five seconds later it fell in the water with a splash, left them wondering how deep the hole was. They'll carve their meat with large knives, stick them in and pull them out, move the food from the back of the throat to the stomach—the noise will be unnerving. I'll put my hands over my ears, see mom and dad's garden, overgrown and deserted, see the three of us carrying keepsake boxes filled to overflowing, and amazing chickens who've learned to make it over the fence and into a tree.

I'll click my tongue. I have to stop. I am not an egg-laying hen! I am not an egg-laying hen!

After dinner I'll help mom make a cake, break eggs in a bowl and whip.

I'll watch my baby girl on the swing. Think how wonderful it must be to be her, lighter than air, floating skyward when left untethered.

How to Skin a Dogfish

K is repeating what they said on the news all morning. I tell him to shut up, "That's not what you heard."

"He grabbed her by the throat," he gasps, hunching over, "ripped it open, ripped it open!"

And Bianca, Bianca is slow as ever. I thought the clatter of dishes would startle her awake. Didn't. I'm afraid she'll be late for school so, rather than yelling up the stairs, I climb up to pull the covers down and drag her to the bathroom to get ready.

Back in the kitchen, I apologize to K. Tell him he was right, *perdonami*. Just because they didn't show torn-out throats, it doesn't mean they weren't there. The whole thing might traumatize him, though. I gotta be more careful because red is not like other colors. Red stays with you.

When Bianca comes down at long last, she'll have an expression of wordless animosity written all over her face, as if she just caught a whiff of dog poop, wondering what dumbass stepped in it. I want to pull her tight against my chest, but she thinks she's too big for that shit so I make her a sandwich instead, tear the lettuce leaves into small pieces, tuck a slice of ham under the cheese. She knows she's cranky. Luckily, breakfast food will make the world a whole lot sunnier.

"Where's *zio* Luigi," she finally speaks, and the skin below my brows stretches. When she was little, she kept asking *dov'è papà, dov'è papà*. I struggled to come up with a plausible explanation so I lied, like I lie to K. The two of them would retreat in some dark corner, hope no one finds them there.

I look at her, then at K, then at her again. Gripping the tablecloth tightly in my hand, I say it's getting chilly, he went outside to chop some wood for the fire. "You want some milk?"

Bianca gives a small nod, "Uh-huh."

From time to time, she slips her hand under her top to check if her breasts have suddenly gotten bigger, then wrinkles her forehead as if to say women need everything men can't give them. Hand between knees, she opens today's newspapers and reads out loud: *A 16-year-old girl severely tortured to death with a sharp-edged weapon.* "Oh, *dio mio!*"

I bend over to say you shouldn't believe everything you read but K shrieks, pleased as a dog chewing on a bone. "Told ya," he can't refrain, "told ya, told ya, told ya!" A weak smile rises to my lips as I lift up my hair. I want to say girls her age are easy to catch—as mackerel. I want it so badly.

Bianca silently agrees, then goes on to tell me I shouldn't worry, "we come wrapped in a thick skin." There's a surprising amount of calmness on her face when she says you need to be damn skilled to peel it off.

"He seemed to have cut deep into her belly," she says scanning the page for the girl's name between bites. After she's taken the spreading knife out of my hand, she turns the wide blade toward her chest.

"Must've sliced away the stomach wall," she says sliding it upward, mouth stuffed with ham, "and under her throat"—I see his Adam's apple thumping, hands digging deep into her flesh—"right through to the back of the neck"—blood squirting all over.

Bianca takes more meat off the plate, swallows it in one go. "It says he left her in the mud, *zia* Ginna, with a gaping hole that was the belly."

"Cut her belly, oh, *dio mio*, oh, *dio mio*!" K screams before I snatch the blade away from her and soak it in the shallow water. I hear the sound of something dropping below the ribcage.

She's finished eating. Picking up her bag, she rises to leave, says she'll be home late tonight, "Don't wait up."

"*Non ti preoccupare*, Ginna," a voice breaks in when she darts forward to give K a kiss on the cheek, top teeth sticking out, "it's nothing serious." It's Luigi, standing at the door, muddy boots on, arm dripping blood like a leaky faucet. His shoulders rise, then hold toward his ears, and I'm thinking his neck is too low on this shirt, some buttons missing, why in the world don't I see his neck?

I hurl Bianca aside.

"Muddy boots!" K croaks, his throat dry with fear. "Oh, *dio mio!*"

He flutters his wings one last time before I cover the cage where he'll be patiently waiting for the lights to change.

Once You Have a Duvet, You'll Be Fine

Aiko

Unknown to her, Aiko's husband would throw a surprise party for her birthday or invite her friends to come stay with them in Okinawa, watch the dormant Kanhizakura buds burst into color. Aiko is crazy about cherry trees, he knows it, but not the most patient person in the world, and the *sakura* is all about waiting. She knows she'll feel like confetti tossed into the air as soon as the first flushes of pink appear, so she waits.

Every year is different when it comes to cherry flowers, though this February they fell too quickly and Aiko wasn't ready. She wasn't ready to stumble about in a flurry of petals, bleeding to death, just yet.

Unknown to her, a letter arrived from court in late January, saying an eviction order had been placed on the house, that she had seven days to leave the property. Her husband stopped paying the mortgage, full of surprises as ever. All the while she waited for him under a tree, blossom-fringed branches bowing toward the ground, as if begging for forgiveness. Waited with bated breath to say *I tried so hard to stop the situation getting this far*, to see what he would say about her leaving him.

The delivery men came in a week to take the sofa, TV, blooms sleeping bright and brittle between the back pages of dog-eared books and all she could say was, "Have you seen the trees?" and they said, "We don't have time for this, ma'am, we're just doing our job."

She thought she could hear a pin drop after they left.

Aiko takes her coat in case the evening is cool. And shoes. She's gonna need comfortable shoes. She's seen people with big scars on their ankles from where they were walking about all the time.

The streets are surprisingly light and spacious. Somewhere in Hokkaido, she knows, the trees are yet to blossom.

Lotte

Lotte's boyfriend shoves his tongue down her throat and, swelling up, says, "You make me so damn hard, baby, I want to bang you until your pussy explodes," then thrusts and grunts while she thanks god almighty she finally found someone who treats her like a naughty little slut. Once he busts a load, she'll wish she was a cat, licking herself to soothe her cracked skin.

Boyfriend's parents lock the door if Lotte tries to run, poke her on her arms and legs with sharp objects—nothing deep, just little pokes to shut her up. When the police came after her friend Maaike had reported her missing, they made her hide in the closet, said, "She lives here no more" and, pants tucked in their boots, went on to obsess about creating a perfect tulip bed, like most Dutch gardeners.

"Tulips are special, *lieve* Lotte," they said when the police officer left. "They are beautiful before the flowers open, will remain so even after they are gone."

Today, they have set their minds to lifting the interior with something colorful and striking. "Nothing makes you feel like you have your house together better than flowers," father says picking up seasonal blooms for the dining room table, home office desk, guest room nightstand, looking for something that will last a bit longer. He draws Lotte's attention to a late bloomer, so big and full it needs extra protection from wind and heavy rain. She watches the sagging skin under his eyes move as he says it's proved excellent for bedding and cutting.

Lotte's lips feel dry and uncomfortable, like they're burning or something. Lotte thinks the irritation will make it hard for her to chew, thinks she'll have to chew slowly, count to 30 with each bite. She wonders if boyfriend will feed her, as always, say *your hair smells so good, baby*, stroking along his mouth, wonders if she should say something.

"This one is our son's favorite," mother resumes, somewhat pensive. "It's undoubtedly a rare beauty, considered a novelty because it's unusual."

Boyfriend sucks his thumb, saliva building up in the corners of his mouth.

They conclude it's a great candidate for forcing, that it will look spectacular in their flower arrangements, then, eyes grim and alert like a raccoon's, point to the long-stemmed tulips next to the front door, "long-lasting, as you might imagine, ideally suited for indoor displays."

Lotte feels like a bug on its back, wonders what to say.

When they aren't looking, she pokes around the rooms, in the flowerpots, in the bushes by the gate, turns things over in hopes of finding the key. Yesterday she noticed a vase is chipped and scratched, thought it needed fixing, and they said, "It's ok, *lieve* Lotte," as if to comfort her, "nothing's broken, why fix it?"

Lotte decides not to say a word.

Tomorrow, Lotte will fall sick. They'll hope it's nothing serious. They'll look worried, they'll believe her. Why wouldn't they? She's delirious, she moans, flows into a rage, sinks into despair, like they do in Russian novels. She hears them squabble, talk about the key. Afraid they might lose her, they'll go fetch the doctor. It strikes Lotte she's gone too far, this may be your only chance, she repeats, don't blow it.

When she *comes round*, they will tell her to rest. They will go away. She will be alone in the room, alone in the house, she will grab a blanket, make her way noiselessly down the stairs, just in case, slip out the door and into the night.

She'll trudge the streets for hours, fall asleep in a doorway, she'll be told to leave in the morning, they'll kick her, stamp on her with their big feet, *you can't sleep here*, they'll say, *go get a job*. She'll plod along. By noon she won't have eaten in two days.

March is closing in, tourists flocking to Holland to see all those colors oozing from the stems. "Look at this elegance, this grace," a tour guide will say, palm holding petals edged with finely cut fringes. The wind will run its fingers along the back of her neck just under her hairline. She'll flinch at its touch as if it were a snake.

Dmitri

The table was set unlike anything I'd seen before: tropical fruit arranged in a wire basket, lighter-toned flowers contrasted with deeper reds and chocolates to create an impressive centerpiece. Last time I got a bed and three meals per day was when I was in jail.

They ask me what's it like and, blade turned in, I say, "Safer than the streets, I was clean for a year, more focused, had a routine."

I wipe my mouth on the back of my hand, fasten my belt tighter, as if trying to squeeze into a crack between two rocks. It's hard to explain to people that I never had dreams. Never knew what I wanted to be, just wanted to be. It's just the way it is for me.

"At night that stuff keeps me warm," I say. "Stops me going la-la in the head."

We smiled, we held hands, shed tears the way roses shed petals. After dinner, they showed me how to make an origami lily, introduce joy one fold at a time, but mine twisted into a rat and swam toward a sewer inlet. Resigned, I sank down on the American leather sofa, fell asleep hugging my knees up to my chin, blanket pulled over my hands to avoid drawing attention to my veins.

You begin to feel it at a young age; your body gives you signs so you damage it once, you damage it twice, too many times to remember. Because you don't know a better way to cope. *Roll with it*, they say, *like a ship in a storm*. I wish I could say, I tried but it didn't work. Truth is, I didn't. Like a letter thrown into the fire, I darkened and curled before bursting into flames.

Back in high school, I'd run away and go missing for weeks. When they kicked me out of ERs, I'd take a long bus ride to keep warm, each time getting on a different bus so drivers wouldn't recognize me. In the morning, I'd walk up to one of the big shopping malls to get changed in the toilet, then sit outside there, lost in thought, faces blowing past. There was this woman, an angel from heaven. She'd come up and say, "Here's a pasty for you, Dmitri," "here's a coffee for you," "I don't want a *спасибо*, sweetheart, just take it."

People used to give me all sorts of things. I had a real nice retro radio back then, but someone stole it when I went off to take a leak in Starbucks. And then I had people call me *tramp* and *druggie*, saying *there should be a law against it*, and stuff. The same people who made me drop out of school when I realized I was gay. I didn't want to hang around there anymore, thought I was big enough to know my old man wouldn't want me either, so just before his second stroke, I left for good. Facing the Neva, I flung my good luck charm into the water and, holding out my hands, palms up, breathed fresh air into my lungs.

The next day, Dmitri felt uneasy, knew they wouldn't say anything inappropriate—they aren't like that—but felt like a burden all the same, like he didn't have the right to peek inside their ensuite bathrooms and balconies, catch a glimpse of what life might have been like. Dmitri saw a couple of friendly faces, Dmitri had a hot shower, washed his clothes, then got right back to where he belongs, like paper flowers that returned to the streets of Campo Maior hundreds of miles from here. Before he sneaked out, with a backpack hiding everything he owns in this world, Dmitri took 1000 rubles from the shoe cabinet after a moment's thought and, coat thrown over his shoulders, pushed the button for the ground floor.

Each day comes as it is. Dmitri feels like he could disappear, and no one would ever know.

Mary Jane, Tech CEO, Dies a Little Every Time Someone Brings Bagels to a Work Meeting

Clutching a bottle of wine, Mary Jane hits the gas and the car lurches forward. The clock tower she drives past tolls 3, 8, 10 times— she shudders at every ring.

At home, she pushes the spoon away, leaves the food spread out on the table. The staircase seems too narrow, too steep to climb so she takes the bottle out to the balcony to finish it and think. With a yellow face, she leans both elbows on the rail to gaze at the last pink flush of the sunset, red circles flashing before her eyes.

Mary Jane loves her job but wants to have a career break to focus on herself. Trouble is, if she reaches for a bagel, they think *there goes the fat boss.* If she doesn't, they silently congratulate her for showing restraint, offering her carrots and granola bars. If M.J. forgets she's fat, the world is there to remind her. Her colleagues talk about the importance of extended family and availability of organic vegetables, regularly giving her tips to make cardio more fun (though it would be easier to buy her smokes to keep her appetite down.) From time to time, it crosses their minds *maybe fat people aren't that bad*.

They don't know you, M.J tells herself, looking at the rapidly changing color of the sky. They don't know what it was like to survive your fat mother, how you stopped taking the bus because she could sense the aggravation of the passengers squeezing past her, how she began obsessing about *your* weight, worrying about you getting fat yourself or, god forbid, ending up blaming your failure on bad luck.

They don't know what it was like to be yet another Honey Boo Boo, how she made you attend beauty contests (although she knew you weren't much of a beauty), and grow long blond hair (because men love girls with soft tanned skin and hair down to their asses), how she paid for your French lessons—*it's always in to speak French*—and how much you hated it, how she had a stroke, how she managed to crawl to the phone, how you unplugged it, how the only thing you remember in French to date is *j'ai tué ma mère*, how the first thing you did after you buried her was chop off your hair.

Out of the blue, Mary Jane would grab a pair of scissors, think, *I feel like cutting again*. The thing about scissors is that you cut your own hair once, then you can't say no to the blades any more.

They tell you *you'll feel better after crying your heart out.* You won't. They don't tell you how they killed their only plant because they forgot to water it, how every evening on their way home from work they buy a package of ice cream and eat it all by themselves.

Mary Jane rubs the back of her neck, feels a lot of tension in her muscles. She bent over the water once but someone happened to walk by so she leaned on a wall of silence, flattened her palms against it.

I never wanted my hair back until recently but it hasn't come back the way I wanted it. Somehow it remains weak and lifeless, no matter what I do to it. So I fill a zip-lock bag with my falling hair, hope it'll grow back someday.

Kristallnacht (*It's Oh So Quiet*)

Father inserted the key blade into the keyhole and twisted the doorknob open. Didn't step in, though. He stood there for a moment, as if his fingers had frozen to the cold metal but bearing it stoically despite the tormenting pain ripping his skin open, sinking into his flesh. He looked detached, somewhat remote when his hand finally loosened the grip.

As he was walking back to the car, I noticed the fluidity of his walk was completely gone, which prevented parts of his body from moving in a sequence of synchronized rhythms. His limbs and trunk appeared disconnected from one other, upper body agonizingly sluggish, like after carrying something heavy, unsure how to change posture, what to do next.

"Don't come in yet," he grimaced at his reflection in the car window. If I didn't know him so well, I'd have thought someone had broken into our house, that he might still be there.

A tall, broad-bodied woman, mother slouched by the car, focusing on smoking the way passionate smokers do, a proper drag involving a number of subtle moves which make the whole thing feel so good.

"Is there something the matter?" she asked in a slow phlegmatic voice, like a visitor from a far-off galaxy who had obviously picked the wrong planet, only half turning her head to look behind.

He scratched his grayish hair where it stuck out from under his hat, then knocked on the window to get my attention. "Stay in the car, I'll come fetch you in five." He uttered something in a low murmur as he walked away.

There's a gap between his upper front teeth that I couldn't see, his lips barely apart when he spoke, like there's a weight on his chest, choking him when he alters his mouth position to project his voice right, so he's made a very conscious decision. My chin knocks against the front seat, stomach feels like a big raw hole where something should be but is not there.

Mother's tummy is full and hard, growing larger by the day. I turn around abruptly, eyes searching to find them crouched behind the car. Nose buried in a grocery bag, she looks like an ostrich nesting, digging shallow holes in the ground for her eggs.

I roll down the window, "Mom, let's go inside." She sticks her lower lip out the way babies do when latching on to their mother or a bottle to soothe them.

"Mom!"

"Ok, ok," she says in a preoccupied manner, round face turning up to the invisible stars.

I get out of the car, taking a brief look at the muddy brown color of the slushy snow around the tires, help her stand up, put the groceries back in the trunk. The cold cuts to the bone. We walk side by side, my keys rattling from a key ring, denim popping between her rubbing thighs. Vast and coppery, the clouds hang inappropriately from the sky, ice crystals cracking underneath like glass shards.

The door is ajar, and we enter the house.

Back against the stone wall, father sits in darkness, unblinking and tired-looking, as though he's hours' drive away from home but not in the mood for driving. The floor is covered with jagged pieces of glass and ceramic tableware—a fine set of cups, drinking glasses, serving dishes, vases and crackled glass decorative plates, taken from the shelves and out of the cupboard, smashed into a million tiny pieces. A loud and clear sound of stepping on sharp-edged glass is heard as we stagger to our feet, stepping on mother's collection of crystal roses and animal heads, my bonsai tree in blossom, father's blown art figurines. Shattered to bits, they look helpless, suddenly too fragile, too delicate to last. It was evidently a violent breaking, yet nothing seems to have been plundered.

Standing motionless, mother and I look across the room, then up at the chandelier suspended on heavy chains. By the time our eyes have reached the top of the stairs, we pant and puff like old steam engines. Wrists covered in blood, my twin sister sits on top of the spiral staircase and, head stuck in the railing, gazes over the edge. She is pallid and still, like a shop-window dummy leaning out onto the street, bare feet dangling in thin air. A broken glass makes no sound, not any more. It just lies there in pieces, scattered round your feet.

The evening of the wake was crystal clear; stars—large and quiet—sparkled like diamonds in the black sky. I pictured her sharpening father's razor to a nice edge, wondered if she suffered. I couldn't help hearing her mumbling something about not wanting to ruin everyone's life over a piece of bread, myself suggesting she should get drunk to wash away her sorrow, then break the glass like a real Serb, squeeze through into the next round.

As the first clods of earth thudded onto the coffin, blood came rushing out of my nose and down my lip, into my mouth. Mother moved her facial muscles as if to smile, tried to find a proper response to *oh J* and *my heart goes out to you* and *terrible loss* while the sun was falling down through the frosted treetops only to disappear silently into the cold cold ground.

Back home, father made a grab at his wrist, pressed hard staring at the floor as if searching for more pieces of the broken glass.

Delivery of Rage

"**G**od damn it, are you even listening to me? It's his fault, Sir, not mine," I told the police officer as the city's belly button was bleeding, the newborn peeking out all sore and ugly.

"Seriously?" the guy giggled under his breath, "I had the right of way, man. I could've hit you."

Eyes narrowed and staring, I gave a quick jerk of my head, brain moving around violently inside my skull, like when there's sudden speeding up and slowing down. "Whatcha talkin' about?" I cried, throwing my hands in the air. "You changed lanes right in front of me, didn't give me a chance to get out of your way. What the fuck is your problem?"

His lips thinned as he pressed them together.

"Cut it out, both of you!" the cop raised his voice, then rubbed his jaw thoughtfully, as if tasting his martini, before taking out an electronic pocket notebook. He navigated the settings easily, square chin turning toward me, "Spill it."

"I was doing about 100, feeling the road under my fingertips, when a black Jeep Cherokee roared past me and swerved to reverse without an indicator. No big deal, I thought. It happens all the time, right? *Wrong!* He turned around, started following me. Took me a couple minutes to realize it."

When I set off for work, the city lay stillborn in the valley's womb, or so it seemed. Next thing you know, a stream of cars is wrapped around its neck like an umbilical cord. The dude is behind me, huffing and puffing. I honk and flash my lights, trying to let him pass. Nothing! So I begin to brake in a *get the hell off my back* manner, but can't really step on the pedal as he'd slam right into me.

He eventually passes me. He's literally a foot away from my bumper but drives at normal speed for miles, and I reckon he came to his senses. I grab a pack from the glove compartment, spank the camel, turn it upside down and, taking a cigarette with my teeth, light up. Suck in, like sucking a milkshake through a straw. I put on some music, the Roxy kind, make a few phone calls, then text wife to tell her *we need to clean our gutters* and *I love you.* But the asshole is glued to me, which really starts to piss me off, so I slow down, watching him drive away until he vanishes from sight, like the shore on a boat trip.

I met him *accidentally* at a drive-thru diner later with curses on his tongue, told him to watch his mouth. He rolls down the window to pick up his order, spits, and, seeing me with a plastic knife, says, "Be careful with that or you'll cut yourself. We'd like to keep you in one life-sized piece, if possible."

A voice whispered to me, *stop breathing, don't exhale*. He flipped the bird, and I lost it. The woman in the passenger seat was screaming something in Chinese. I told her to fuck off. Damn immigrants, always picking a fight!

We got out of the trucks with our fists up.

The cop puts the electronic notebook back in his pocket and, making sure the buttons on his shirt are done all the way up, reaches for the handcuffs.

"You psycho!" I yell, nostrils flaring, jail sentence dangling from my bloody wrists, "why couldn't you let go?"

"Yeah?" he draws hot air in through his teeth, hands trembling in the metal rings, "why couldn't you?"

Meaning of the Color Black

Determined not to say anything to anyone yet, I dragged myself to work after a couple of days off and the first thing I asked my 50-something Montreal-based colleague Martha was *how's Judy?* I'd met her at a Christmas party a few years before— sweet kiddo, narrow at the waist and *slim like a birch*, I told her mother, her lips curling into a grin.

"Her father was nicely built back in the day. When I was her age, though," she looked at Judy, her face changing shape suddenly, "children got the birch when they misbehaved."

"Yes, ma'am," the girl lowered her head, appearing small. For a split second I thought she was serious, but then she winked mischievously at me and I knew she'd be one of the cool kids everyone envies.

"Growing up, you know," Martha moved her eyes in a circle. "She broke up with her boyfriend last month."

"Oh! That's too bad. It must be hard on you."

"He told her, 'I'm a better person when I'm with you, you're unlike anyone I've met.' Men! Yeah, I guess. *C'est la vie.* Yourself?"

I wanted to say something funny but couldn't bring myself to say it. The sun was cutting through the sky, a dazzling white light making it almost impossible to keep my eyes open.

"I'm burying Daniel tomorrow," I muttered, and I swear she had the same expression as my big brother Ted when he barged through the door without knocking to ask about my secret crush on his best friend Danny. D moved to Toronto from southern England after his dad had passed and mom found a new job. I still hate the dark days of winter here. He didn't mind the cold.

"It's true what they say, isn't it?" Ted raised his eyebrows, his wild hair askew. I twisted my face like I didn't care, chewing on my pencil that was turning to sand in my mouth.

"What are you talking about?" I say, scanning his face, looking for signs of what he was thinking, silence between us like a letter slipped under the door—impatient to be torn open, show what's inside.

"Danny and you." Ted enjoys the game, without feeling the slightest bit guilty for letting me sweat.

"Danny and *me*? Are you fucking kidding me?"

"Oh cut the crap, you blushed."

I dragged my feet over the edge of the bed. "And?"

"Aaand you're *so* in love with him, you can't even hide it, can you?"

"Get the fuck out! Can't you see I'm studying?"

"I will if you admit it."

"Admit what?"

He grabbed my waist and threw me down on the bed. Wouldn't let go until I said yes.

"Just so you know," he said with the doorknob in his hand, imitating the British accent, "I believe him to be the finest young man in the whole frigging world, pardon my French."

I stuck my tongue out at him. Then he left.

I remember how pissed I was when he told Danny, and mom and dad, and everyone on the street, and just about everyone I knew. Stupid fuck! He always had to open his big mouth.

"Why couldn't you keep it between us?" I said. He leaned his head to one side, slightly open lips exposing a fine set of snow-white teeth.

"Tess," he asked later that day, facing the roses growing up against the wall, arm wrapped around my shoulder, "do girls know when guys check out their ass?"

"I don't have ass radar to tell me every single time a guy's got his eye on it but yeah, we know."

"I...I—" Martha stuttered, blinking into the morning sun, "don't even know what to say," which I found hard to believe because she always had something to say, to someone else, that is.

"*C'est la vie—merde*. Between you and me"—I was hardly restraining my tears, getting all choked up—"I don't want anyone to know just yet. I couldn't stand people pitying me now. Please!"

She shrank like a cooked tomato. Stood there goggle-eyed, mouth like a cave, as I stepped into the office.

Inside, I put the coffee down, flop my skinny ass on the chair. Danny's face on the mahogany desk catches me off-guard. I'm like a rabbit on the road, mesmerized by the beam of the car's headlights. I find him in the cup today, in the herbs on the windowsill, in the walls, the shade. Danny in a dark-colored flannel shirt and Doc Martens, started growing a beard. Our first kiss (intimidating)—how much tongue do I use/ does my breath smell bad/ where do I put my hands? We bump heads, unsure which way to turn them. First time he picked me up in his mom's baby blue sedan—when midnight struck, he drove me back home. His first motorbike—leather pants and a black jacket. "Big thrills come with big risks," his mom says, giving us helmets. She was pretty—rusty-red hair and high cheekbones, straight-backed like a dancer, a 'wide awake and ready for whatever life throws at you' kind of person. I feel I can trust her. Her beige dress suits her perfectly. She lowers her eyes to check out my skirt, must be thinking *'it's too sexy for a motorcycle'*. (She's probably right.) I'm leaning with Danny— am I leaning too much/ too little? First time I told him I loved him—it felt awkward, like speaking in public for the first time. (I can't stop looking at his little pink dimples bobbing up and down.) First dinner at my parents'—I fumble around in my purse for the keys while he kisses my neck. Our first fuck— that car, that summer—Danny unbuttons his stonewashed jeans, adjusts them on his hips when he gets out. First time I saw him on his knees—his hair keeps flopping over his eyes. "Will you?" He looks enthusiastic about the idea. Just a random picture of the lake I took when I left work earlier so we could have a fuck. He's adorable—thick hair, freckles and V-neck sweaters. I'm tall, look like a bony fillet of fish. "I love your bones," he said, then we fucked again. He begged me to leave my job that day, which I did. Wanted me to become somebody, and I did. Our last fuck a few days ago, with the sky growing pale above, roots hard under our backs—Danny touches the bone above my breasts, "Do you know the clavicle is one of the most commonly fractured bones?" Last picture— Danny, with a fractured skull and broken collarbone, pressing his nose into mine. He fell riding his motorbike. I try to smile away my tears but shrink from the sight of blood on his chest. "It's nothing," he's quietly confident, "don't worry." We spend the evening in bed after I let everyone know he's safe and well and on the mend. I kiss his head while he has a torn blood vessel in the brain somewhere which slowly forms a clot. When I left him in the morgue, I felt my heart beating in my stomach. The house was silent and dark, so dark I had to feel my way along the walls to the bedroom door.

All giddy and disoriented, I plug the office phone in to call my brother.

"Ted?"

"Yes, Tess?"

"Last time he shaved, I asked him if I could do it and he let me, but the razor slipped and I cut him. He was the brave one, and then at the hospital, his hands jittered while mine stayed steady. Funny, isn't it?"

I hear Ted breathing.

"They are shaped differently. Did you know that?"

"What, Tess?"

"Coffins are wide at the shoulders. 'You must have seen them in cowboy movies.' Mr. Kirk was patient with me. I pretended I remembered. They accept all types of payment, credit cards and all. I might as well choose something pricey, something memorable—like a $3,000 vacuum-sealed, navy blue metal casket with steel handles—what do you say?"

"What difference does it make when you're gone?"

"The lower-end models begin at $999. You can purchase them in Walmart these days, you know."

I gulp down the last of my coffee which feels like a large chunk of melon stuck in my throat.

"Mr. Kirk doesn't do caskets but will be generous to provide a scattering over Lake Ontario at no extra cost if I opt for cremation. It's cheaper."

I swallow again. "What does the Bible say about cremation, Ted?"

"Buried in weakness, raised in strength," he responds quickly as though he's doing one of those answer-without-thinking psych tests, and we both chuckle.

"Clothing is optional, from what I hear. If there's no service, you can be cremated in whatever you passed away in— PJs or a hospital gown. Holy shit, Ted! We could make a tunic out of it, secure it with pins at the shoulder.

"Like the old Greeks."

"Yep, like the old Greeks."

"Cremation freaks me out, Tess."

"Me too. I don't like the idea of his bones turning into ashes—his thighbone, arm bones, pieces of his hip, skull, his fingers and toes and all the little bones charring in the fire. 'It comes out the consistency of soft sand,' Mr. Kirk said, he'd most likely look like tanned Florida beaches. How cool is that!"

"He deserves a proper burial, Tess."

"He does. I'll tell them to put him deep in the ground so he can smile longer. They haven't mentioned coping mechanisms, though. What do you do till the bones turn dry and brittle, huh?"

"Tess?"

My eyes begin to sting. I struggle to breathe.

"Remember when we were little?"

"What?"

"We made believe we were pirates."

"Yeah. That was fun."

"And when the lights went off, I was scared shitless, had to grope my way up the dark stairs to find you."

I'm thinking about the full meaning of smile.

The cold pierced my bones the previous night. I tried to shake off the chill, sticking to my shoulders like dandruff, scrape it like mud off my cold feet. Couldn't. The heating had broken down and the technician never showed up. In bed, my skin felt ashy and untouched. I couldn't stop itching. Fell asleep with three blankets on top of me. The winter's heartwarming today. It'll stay warm throughout the week.

"It should be overcast and windy, the sky throat-choking, unforgiving. It's too fucking cheerful for the funeral, Ted."

"I know, sweets, I know."

I look out the window, feel my bones pressing the nerves. Is this how a tree leaning over the cliff feels, heavy branches bending under their weight? Noise bleeds out front, in the sidewalk cracks coated with thick layers of dust, on the boulevards crushing worlds in their sweaty palms. Skulls grin at each other, chatting of this and that on the steps of the coffee shops, waiting humbly in line to get into the cool new restaurants, eye sockets black and hollow like concrete blocks, a supersized soda and supersized fries next to a dumpster. Cars hurtle by, squeal to a stop, window washers make the dirty glass clean, postmen deliver mail, volcanoes erupt, plates shift, the universe expands. The sun touches me through the curtains—Danny's hands between my legs.

Pain Is Part of the Process

"Listen up, scumbags!" the warden growled, routinely strip-searching me and other inmates for tattoos. "Your body is no longer yours. Your body belongs to the state now."

When the lights went out, the whole jail chanted *fish fish fish!*

***

Carefully, he peeked through the glass window in the door before coming in. Sounded like a real estate agent recruiting new people, inquired about our experience, client reviews and stuff. And when he complimented me on my studio, calling it lofty and well-proportioned like it was a Victorian house, I couldn't tell if that was a good thing so I just lifted my gaze in a *what can I do for you* manner and smiled politely.

He seemed to know a lot about me. Knew I started tattooing behind bars, knew I kept my needles, I washed the guns clean, kept my own ink. He was obviously in the mood for talking. Me, I thought, what the heck! He's a client, you gotta be nice to your clients.

Sterilizing equipment, I tell him I stole bikes at 12, cars at 13, then moved on to stores and homes. At 15, I joined a gang. We robbed a business and it went bad, someone got shot, which sent me to prison for eleven and a half years. He confides he robbed a restaurant, earning himself six years in close security. Now he wants barbed wire around his neck, shows me the design. It's large, it will need lots of coloring and shading. The dude doesn't know shit. He would love to think of himself as a sword swallower but has yet to learn how to hold all those blades in his throat. Soon everything will be clear as day.

"You gotta learn the ropes quickly, don't you?" he's curious, leaning against the counter, looking behind me where all the gear is kept, nods as if to say the shop is clean and unintimidating, and I nod back.

"What works for you on the outside, you learn to bring inside. The only thing different is you don't have a gun—you use your hands instead." I roll up my sleeve to show him my first tat, dating back to the 90s when I was locked up in a juvenile detention center. You do the first one to let others know who they're dealing with. You do all the rest because you can't stop. After a while, your skin can't take it anymore, and you keep doing it because everybody else does it. I got my arms done, got my chest done, my back. It's the classic bad boy look but no matter how beautiful each new one looks after it's been inked onto your body, it's what happens next that really counts.

"We'd scrape bits off our heels with a blade, burn the pieces under glass, then dissolve it in piss," I add, telling him to lay back. I'll quickly do a stencil of the tattoo before transferring it to his neck, but first I need to clean the area with alcohol and shave it to make sure there are no hairs to get in the way.

"And then what?" The guy stares in terror as if I just pointed a knife at him, not sure what to expect.

I twist my mouth into a strange smile. "Then you wrap it up with toilet paper, hope there's a God."

When I saw I could make good use of my hands, I made myself a gun. I got the wheel, I got the ink, the needle—that's all I needed to set a new course. With time, I learned to use anything I could grab hold of—ballpoint pens, paint stolen from the jail paint store, cigarette ash. Of course ninja turtles knew what we were doing. They'd open the doors in the middle of the night, make us step off the bunks. They'd strip us naked, open grates, take out mats to have them x-rayed. I knew I could end up in a dungeon, like I knew it's a skill that would keep me from making myself a target more than necessary, so I needed to be super cautious.

After I put on the gloves, I get the ink ready, placing the needles into the tattooing machine.

"What does it feel like?" he asks.

"What?"

"The needle."

"Like a cat dragging its claws across your skin," I say with grim determination, the tattoo gun moving across his skin, "and the cat will scratch more if you make her mad—try not to breathe."

He clenches his jaw. His neck throbs, leg shakes by itself. "And the prison? Like hundreds of needles poking deep into your flesh, huh?"

"The first night you won't be able to sleep a wink coz your bunky will be spanking his monkey all night long."

He raises his upper lip as if he just saw his former boss outside the window, then glowers at a cab that's come to a noisy stop at the light.

"When you get a care package from your baby mama," I say readjusting the needle, "you'll know."

Papayas Gone Bad

So I was on the bus back home the other night when this guy gets on with the bluest eyes you've ever frickin' seen. He looks at me and my jaw hits the floor. I swear to you on my mother's grave I got the urge to climb on top of him and never get off of him. *Ever!*

Bullets of water are pelting down and there's like a million people inside, dripping with sweat, touching me with their smelly bodies. It reeks of sickness. Ugh! It's like spoilt papayas, their skin changing color in the areas of rot, like that time when my suitcase with a papaya in it was lost and found at an airport other than mine after a month. I could feel the vomit-like stench on my clothes for months.

Anyway, it's pitch-black outside, you can't see a thing out the windows, and I'm wearing that super-hot T with my cleavage exposed and all, and I'm like *oh my god*, the fucker's staring at my boobs!

Very organic-looking, he pushes his way toward me, then presses close against me, his bedraggled clothes sticking to my skin, water spreading out into a pancake between us. The woman next to me begins to freak out coz she can't breathe as I feel him growing like a papaya tree in blossom, hands flat on the window.

I left a pile of dishes in the sink so I apologize for the mess as we walk into the kitchen, roll up my sleeves and get busy. A steady rain is pouring from the faucet. He feels perfectly ripe reaching for my suds-covered hands, holds them up later in the shower, pushing against me, sinking into my skin the way the sun spills its breath in the rain. He moans in my throat, tastes healthy in my mouth, like a squeeze of lime on a fresh papaya. The following morning, we scoop out the fruit of the angels in bed, somewhere in Hawaii, maybe Mexico.

"What is it, baby?" he asks. "You seem worried."

"How can this beautiful piece of fruit go bad when it otherwise looks and feels so good?"

"It's natural," he replies. "All papayas eventually go bad."

My chest tightens, voice is edgier. "They do, don't they?"

"I mean, unless you eat them on time, which is why we're not going to wait."

I stare at an uncut half in my hand, eyes circling its rim, ask how he knows when a papaya is ripe. Taking it out of my hand, he strokes it tenderly for a while before inserting a sharp blade into its flesh. He turns it upside down, lets the seeds bleed out into the bowl. The extra stubborn ones refuse to let go. He has to force them out with his fingers.

"You can tell from the slight orange blush on its skin," he says pinching my cheek, grabs the biggest piece, bites it in two.

My hand moves toward my neck but changes direction suddenly to cover the belly. The air feels like a velvet dress today—heavy and uncomfortable. Soon there will be rain and fog and cloud.

The bus pulls into the bus stop, the doors open, then slam with a loud bang. The blossom drops and the fucker's *gone*!

Whoa, did you just see that? I clapped and the lights turned off.

Wasps Don't Die After One Sting

Half an hour later, mom's in the hallway, gazing out the window. It's springtime, the back garden teeming with life. She takes an unopened pack of cigarettes out of her purse, rolls it in her hands some and, making sure she's read that part about the increased risk of cancer and heart disease, raps it several times against her palm. She likes tobacco tighter in the paper so she can smoke longer. Pop-eyed and forlorn, like a tourist sightseeing, I walk down the warren of narrow streets, looking up, looking down, checking out the arrows and peeking into exam rooms where doctors with odd names and expensive questions are supposed to help people like me, like us—a pile of mismatched parts whose deepest fear is that of the light.

They call it a Help Center for Minors, though everyone knows it's a madhouse. Even I do, despite being *too young to understand*. I'll be kept in for observation, I'm sure of it. In the meantime, I was given little squares of white with a streak of pink, as well as once yellow suns, removed from each other to form crescent moons and yeah, I need to report twice a week after preschool.

Inside, mom planted herself in the seat next to me, placing her hands on the armrests as a long-legged woman and two men—one tall, one short—took turns interrogating me. They got off to a slow start, avoiding cringe-worthy phrases and catching their breath at the question mark, but not long after picked up speed, like detectives who work at different sites to uncover every clue. Asked *what does it feel like*, this explosion of itching, burning and biting all over my body, *where do you feel it* and *can you compare it to something familiar*, asked kid things, grown-up things, things about mom—gripping the carved balls at the ends—things about dad, his blood in mine and such, about mom and dad—although I don't know anything about him or them for that matter, so I couldn't answer those—things about things.

"Like being stabbed with dozens of daggers and bayonets," I said, my skin roaring, inhabited, after which Beanpole wanted me to expose it.

I brushed my cheek with my fingertips, instinctively drawing my chair away as if from the fire but mom said *don't*, then helped pull my shirt up, their eyes leaning over to have a closer look, flashing, circling, scrutinizing my cuts and wounds one by one, inside and out, comparing the left to the right ones, the upper to the lower ones the way insurance agents inspect the damage caused by the storm, my throat giving a loud cry of pain every time their pupils touched my body.

"Grazes should be covered with a waterproof dressing until a scab forms," Shorty suggested, arms crossed over the chest. I couldn't help but wonder if Beanpole's look meant *you'll be ok* or *time will tell what we currently can't.*

"Doctors bandaged me once but flesh is too tempting to resist," I said, then went on to straighten my shirt. "Some areas on my back I can't even reach—if I could, I'd scratch them too—others got so numb that my fingernails can go through the skin. I'd scratch through the skull all the way into my brain if ..." I stopped for a brief moment to rub my hair with a paper napkin. "Everywhere, it itches everywhere, and I have no idea when it started, really," I said before even being asked. "I remember trying to scratch it off—the itch wouldn't go away. Oddly, it seems to have been with me forever. Without it, I'd feel awkward, incomplete, don't know, it's like it belongs there," I uttered in the same breath, the corners of my mouth drooping as if seeking sympathy, and they just probed me further.

"Have you seen someone about it, tried some remedies to reduce discomfort?" one of them asked. I watched all three break eye contact to put their pens down. Nodding, I glanced at mom. She gave me the *I'm talking to you* look, though, so I carried on.

"Come to think of it, it might have been in the backyard that I first felt it, like the one you have here"—I point in the direction of the open window—"because I thought at some point I'd unintentionally disturbed a wasp nest, brushing my hand against a stinging nettle. Next thing you know, little savages are all over my limbs, my back, face, injecting their bodies under my skin. I flail my arms around to get them off of me, desperately try not to fall...Yes," I say, after a brief pause, staring at mom again—"an array of experts. We," my voice cracks, "tried...just about everything."

This time she does the nodding part, hand slightly covering her mouth.

Leggy looks like she just joined a contemplative order of nuns, as if I wasn't there, as if none of us was, as if she ran out of questions or had nothing to declare.

"Have you tried ignoring it, Charlie?" Beanpole asks. I do what Leggy just did. I rub my brow, fingers sliding across the temple and over the ear to stroke the back of my neck.

I sound much older. I know it. They know it.

"He prefers going by his formal name," mom speaks at last. "It's Charles, not Charlie."

"Charles?" he repeats.

"You can ignore the itch, not the stinging frenzy," I shrug, pulling on my sleeves. "Wasps aren't fooled when you play dead."

"Of course not," he smiles stingily, after which he'll dig into his pocket to take out another pen, a different-colored one.

They tell us we should take a short break, allow me to catch my breath and freshen up before we resume the conversation. Moving away from the desk, mom begins to shake out her legs the way boxers do before or during a match, says they feel sore again. Wooden almost. I don't know how she can do it here. The room is so tiny even I can't stretch out fully standing up.

When we step outside, I open a bottle of orange juice to take a sip. It's cold and sweet in the back of my throat as I roll a thought in my head. Mrs. Lila, our downstairs neighbor, was the first to see my galaxy of scars. Mom feels comfortable around her, though I think she confides to way too many people. Then again, Mrs. Lila might be the only one who doesn't make fun of mom's promiscuity, which is yet another word I had to google after I'd heard it roll off a mutual friend's tongue—*someone who has lots of romantic partners*. It's just that I haven't noticed anything romantic about them. I asked once if any of the men she'd been bringing home was my dad. "No," she said, "why do you ask?"

I hear her sigh now, mouth twitching, yellow fingers curling up like old letters, and the tingling starts all over again, my arms aching, feet feeling tight and swollen. I take another swallow of my juice, then close my eyes.

Sometimes I see Daddy serving himself from an enchilada buffet at a suburban Mexican restaurant, chicken on his plate cut into bite-sized pieces, hot sauce stains on his shirt. When he wins a scratch card, he takes me out to buy me brightly-colored fun. We fly together, defying gravity. Sometimes he teaches me to do a tap dance before bed. I want to follow his subtle lead, afraid I'm going to step on him. *He's a great dancer, isn't he?* I tell mom as Daddy puts me on his large feet. *This is how he knocked me off my feet*, she grins. *That's a good one, mom*, I say, watching her move the coffee table out of the way while Daddy rolls up the rug and, eyes shining, we dance, we dance. *I wish this would never end*, I say in a subdued voice before I fall asleep in their arms.

When Daddy takes a shower in the morning, the whole house fogs up. *Work has mom stressed out*, he says watching her pinch the cigarette tightly, sucking on it so hard it squeaks. *Patients can be disgusting and abusive. She needs something to take the edge off.* After he throws on some jeans, he leaves little heart drawings on the cloudy mirror. Later in the day, we put up a tent in the backyard, the smell of crushed grass under our feet. He shows me how to build a fire to chase the wasps and yellow jackets away. *Dad*, I sound certain, *they'll just get angrier.* He scoffs, calls them pretentious. *If you can't beat them, boy, make friends with them. Hey wasps,* he shouts at the top of his lungs, *how about something sugary? You love fruit desserts, don't you?* Daddy takes a big bite out of an apple, then spins what's left of it into the air like a coin. *The more rotten, the better, right? Right,* I wholeheartedly agree, tossing mine into the fire, like a big chunk of wood that will burn all night. We leave the rear door open when we get back inside, letting the sweet scent of apples drift through the house. I take off my shoes, walking across the room on tiptoe not to wake mom, but Daddy tells me never to sneak in, *sometimes they arrest you for trespassing. And don't you worry,* he sounds as though he has a sword on his hips, *there comes a time when wasps stop being hungry.* We fall asleep in my bed, foreheads pressed together, mouths set in a goofy smile.

Sharp voices calling out my name startle me awake. Seconds later, mom and I are back in the room with a sterile shine. I flick a glance at the plant by the door, leaf tips wilted and brown, wonder how long it can go without water before it's pronounced dead. In the corner, a bonny creature dangles from a metal stand—all bones, robust bones, supportive and protective bones, bones that will become thinner, stiffer, limiting bones, bones that will make us shorter, become a burden, bones that are already too heavy to carry, mom explained once.

Sometimes I see him in strangers on the subway. He holds a hose, wearing flame-resistant clothing, or sits in a high umpire chair, announces the score, or that of a senior corporate executive. Other times he drives drunk passengers around, offers smiles and small talks, or he's just a guy you walk by on a street—the one that spits on his hand, rubbing his palms before going to check out a dollar menu. One day he's an out-of-town bore, chewing greasy popcorn at a multiplex, when his skin starts to itch all over. He tries hard not to disturb his wife and boys who gaze up, obliviously, at Harry Potter so he goes on pretending. But not for long. He has to rub, writhe, curse. Rub, writhe, curse. *The theater has fleas in the seats*, he decides. *It must be fleas*. Within days, odd marks begin to appear on his body. Red ones. Little round things raised from his skin like volcanoes.

There's a glimmer of the sun on distant hills as Shorty's voice breaks through silence. "Can we go on? We'd like to ask you something about Charles' father," he says facing mom. She stares long at her hands, pursing her lips in thought, scowls every now and then like a teenage girl who refuses to say anything.

"Do we really have to go into that?" she eventually says.

"We're afraid we do, ma'am," all three confirm, asking her how she feels.

She pinches the bridge of her nose, tries to focus her thoughts.

"Pretty much like ending it," she states quietly.

"Have you talked to someone about it?"

"No."

A long pause.

"Suic—" She stops herself. "Things like that add a mental angle."

Sometimes he's just a face reflected in water, disappearing into the depths at the first drop of rain.

Mom looks at me with wet, sorry eyes. "Some itches are impossible to scratch," she says, as if a knife curled in the pit of her stomach.

Not wholly convinced, I dig my nails into the piece of skin just below the belly and scoop. All of a sudden, I'm not so sure.

I Don't Bleed When You Cut Me

When my bestie and I made a blood pact, I felt irritated and strangely fragile. I saw it in Hollywood once. Kevin Kostner takes out a pocket knife, cuts his hand right there. Robin Hood apparently didn't disinfect the blade first so I figured his hand probably needed amputation. My hands don't heal well. What if—? I thought.

She sits behind me in high school. Prods my back with a ruler to tell me all about the boy. I roll my eyes, fighting to keep my fingernails from scratching my face. Outwardly, she's like a kiwi—rough to the touch. I am smooth on the outside but appearances can be deceiving.

Our hands are twisted into a tight knot when we scab for money, despised for the things we haven't done. Inside, we darken our eyelids and drink cheap beer from the bottle, flipping through teen magazines, snap a quick photo of a world that has built its walls too high before crawling back into our skin. There isn't a single restaurant worth waiting in line for, we conclude, chewing skinny mac n' cheese on the floor.

We stuck with one another through thick and thin, and she reassured me that having our blood running through each other's veins would be the right thing to do. You don't make a pact with someone you don't plan on staying with for life. I reassured myself there are worse things than an open wound, tried to picture how cool I'd look with a new scar. I'd imagined it the old-fashioned way, though—pricking thumbs, pressing them together and saying something terribly important, like *till the end of time and beyond.*

"I'm not a diabetic," she says, cutting us with her father's claw-sharp razor blade, just above the bone that sticks out of the wrist, then rubs her blood into my skin and licks us clean, her tongue disappearing in my flesh like the deepest diving fish on record before leaping in the air again. We're salty and weightless.

It felt like nail clipping. I thought it would hurt. It didn't. It's the idea of pain that I find much worse than the pain itself. Someday I might be brave enough to not be afraid of pain anymore.

The Reason I'm Calling Is to Tell You I'm Gone

Pale and small, Vincent sits on the front porch, paper boat in his lap, smiling as if it were a repetitive task, not much different from washing or ironing. He stares at the street lined with lampposts that spread like stains over the evening sky, thinks *what a great way to fight the darkness*. The dust-coated hedges and lawns look less alive in the fading sunlight, though *less alive* is better than *no longer alive*, because they'll come to life tomorrow and the day after—the severed nerves in his leg won't. They are forever dead, the rest of his body like the lampshade by his side—so dirty you can't see the light.

***

Vincent is a boy. The boy dreams of being a real man, because real men know life in the military isn't for everyone when dropping uniform tops to pile up sandbags, because every soldier has to spend every damn moment jumping out of their own butt just to keep up. So when Vincent plays soldiers with his best friend Logan, he knows already they ain't just anyone.

Vincent's mother says, "Of course it's possible to make one person better off without making the other person worse off." Vincent's father doesn't think so, but Vincent's father carries an umbrella when it rains—and Vincent doesn't. Because officers don't carry umbrellas, because *I am not my father. I want to serve my country*, Vincent tells himself raking the leaves together, laying them against the wall. *I want to serve.*

***

Logan says each time your chin crosses the bar's threshold, your physical fitness test score looks better, more mature. Vincent is a fast learner, he learns fast. He learns from his friend who's given up on his dreams, learns that extra weight can hold you down while trying to pull yourself up, so he sheds all things unnecessary he was used to dragging along and presses on. Soldiers bring God to the field, and God is the only one he'll bring along once he becomes a soldier. He learns from his father who strips him naked, covers him in blood, "coz we didn't fight in 'Nam or World War II, we don't know the Pacific and the Atlantic, there's no one to follow into the military—you'll never make it." He learns from himself, crouched in the shadows, firm in silence as the ladder he's climbing is firm, from goggling his eyes on teachers, from being pulled by the ears to the punishing corner. He learns from dorks who jack gear in the squad, order fancy food when you pick up the tab, the repeaters scared to death of their own mediocrity, and good guys hanging pictures of their wives' bellies, calling them after they've put Chloes and Mikes down for a nap. He learns from his asshole instructor hurling insults, learns that pain is part of the drill—"it toughens you up, makes a man out of you." He learns from the people he'll outrank, learns not to bend easily into a different shape.

***

When Vincent lands in the dark of Afghanistan—ugly, but not the way he imagined—he'll fall into a muddy field, wade through deep grass, boots and pants covered in muck.

Day after day, Vincent will drink coffee from a paper cup, followed by yet another sunset. The silence will be exhausting.

In a month's time, he'll start dreading what every soldier dreads—that the whole deployment will be so uneventful he'll have nothing to tell when he gets back. Vincent knows battles aren't about winning or losing. He just wants to get into the war, to fight, to show them how to build democracy, or something like that. Figures he'll make sense of it all when he gets home. If he gets home. But he doesn't think about that much either. After all, he doesn't have a wife waiting for him, like she'll never receive the call every military spouse prays she'll never get (the one that starts with *Ma'am, I need you to sit down*), or listen to the thunderstorm breaking and crashing as she receives the folded flag, the one who won't fall to her knees in front of everyone, who'll do it when the gate bangs shut.

***

Soon, very soon, Vincent will be moving through the villages, and burning poppy fields, and blowing tunnels, and shooting chickens, and raising the stars and stripes. When you get back, Vincent thinks, eyes moist and shining, sweaty palms will clap *he's the man, he's the man.* "Pages of history," his battalion commander will say after he's shot a rocket into the wrong house. "Pages of history," after killing a family of six in an attempt to gain control, when he gains control.

Vincent shuts his eyes, wants to disappear. He dreams of girls in dotted red dresses, whose eyes twinkle like the lights beyond the desert, nails digging deep into his back. He sees soldiers proposing in the same bars where they met. Their girlfriends cry, everyone cries. Soldiers do too after being dumped for another soldier. Vincent is a realist. He doesn't bitch about the winds—he adjusts the sails. Vincent dreams of a girl he had the hots for in high school, the one who thought him a perv, who used to sulk all day before sticking her fleshy tongue into his mouth, the one who probably doesn't remember him. He knows winning her over would be next to impossible, but dreams are the only place he wants to be.

Vincent hopes he'll eventually marry the girl next door, flat and one-dimensional as a Japanese painting, the one who weeps all the way through the movie and excuses herself when rising from the table, lips curved in a refined smile. He dreams of her naked, fingers clutching at the sheets, dreams of her dreaming of men who lean over you when saying *I will always love you, stay with me, I will always love you.* "Pages of history, soldier," after he gives cash to the relatives who've remained, "you must feel like a God."

Vincent picks up the phone, knows not who to call.

***

Vincent will be thinking about the girl next door, rosy-cheeked and unmoving like a doll, while he gets shot at from all directions, feeling as if he's fighting the whole country alone. And he'll forget what he's learned when a blast of heated air rushes past. He'll forget to be afraid and "the more afraid you are," his drill instructor would say, "the better you're able to handle emergency situations."

When the shooting finally stops, Vincent won't feel a thing. The girl next door lays her index finger against his lips, says *shhh, I will always love you* before an awkward silence falls, and his eyes fall—but not the way he imagined.

He sees his father, black band sewn on his jacket, strangers rolling up his clothes, throwing them into a bag. He hears the girl next door say *I want to clean him up before his mom sees him. Silly*, she says, *it's all I can think of*, then picks up his uniform off the floor, puts it on her chest.

When they find him, he'll be sprawled on the side of a canal with metal in his limbs, body all tangled up. The roadside bombs will go on exploding, somewhere. Soldiers will go on finding them before they go off, sometimes.

There will be blood, lots of blood. They'll let the girl know there's shrapnel damage, *we're not sure of the extent. Again, he's alive, but he's critical.*

He'll be given morphine. He'll sleep.

He'll dream of reds and blacks, piles of corpses— deleted and retrieved like application data—tripping and falling. His drill inspector saying, "Don't try to understand the Afghans, they'll hate you anyway." *Your father's hair turned white overnight*, his mother will say, holding a tray of heart-shaped cookies, focused on the sound her heart is making under her ribcage. You drop your ass down, put your feet up, you'll remember...then all a blur.

He'll feel numb in one shoe when he awakens. And famished. He'll want to eat, and he will—double his usual amount. They'll flash him a thumbs up. They'll tell him "we're sending you home." They'll tell him "you'll get a medal, there will be an HBO documentary, we'll watch you on YouTube."

You're a tin soldier standing on one leg, he'll think that day and the day after—not enough metal to make you whole.

***

He'll be given a wheelchair when he gets his hands moving again. The wheelchair will take him somewhere (where he doesn't want to go), but he's going nowhere. In bed, he'll wonder how the fuck to rid his skin of dirt. "Mom," he'll say in his sleep, "you can't possibly make one person better off without making the other person worse off."

There are cardboard boxed stacked on the floor. He's going home.

***

Back home, you won't put your pants on one leg at a time, just like everyone else. You'll tuck plurals in, fold anything excess against your body. The neighbors will hear things breaking, flying out the windows—sounds so sharp they could bore a hole in the ground.

Sleeves rolled up to the elbow, you'll grip the table edge at the bar, smash the beer bottle against it, threaten to kill everyone.

Back home, you'll buy a knife to survive.

People will talk in languages you won't be able to understand, countless syllables pouring out of mouths, like after burning your tongue with hot milk. The voices will stop when you draw near.

In the morning, your mother will point to your wheelchair. "Can't be that hard, can it?" she'll say, glancing over toward the forest, path cutting through the dense trees. "Push push glide, push push glide—like ice skating." In the evening, she'll point to your plate, "He's barely touched his food." Hands sunk deep in the pockets, your father will look as though he's sleeping deeply. Every so often, he'll take them out to rub his face, as if to say *I see no point going on*.

You'll toss that knife in the trash, become silent, as silent as stone is silent—or your father.

Back home, you'll dream of me, thin and light as a paper boat, before I get carried by the wind and you decide to stop with that nonsense, "stop it already!" You'll stare at the fire, think it might be a good ending if you were consumed by the flames, like the tin soldier. It's just that tin soldiers don't melt into the shape of little tin hearts. When you find them, they are burned black as coal.

Something That Will Blow in the Wind

That spring, a pigeon laid a couple of eggs on my balcony between gerbera daisies and marigolds. For a while, I thought I should do something about it—anything is better than nothing—but soon realized whatever that *something* was, it wouldn't be right so I left them there and went out of town in hopes that Mother Nature would take better care of it. In my dream, I threw them off the balcony to see them return in the fridge. Then I made scrambled eggs for breakfast.

By the time I got back, the babies had already hatched. Nasty-looking chicks the size of a baby's ass killed all of my plants and shitted all over the place. There were bird droppings on my chair, my lamp fixture, the walls and floor tiles.

I could say now I didn't have the heart to dispose of them. But it's not how I felt. I threw up. That's how disgusted I was. And scared as hell. Don't know why. I just was.

It took me days to clean up. When I finally did, I locked the balcony door and pulled back the covers, thought of giving them some time to grow up, fly away when ready.

As time went by, the birds got bigger and bigger although I never saw their mother feeding them. I liked to believe they were left to their own devices. Somehow it was easier to blame the irresponsible pigeon-parent, and let nature run its course.

"This is what happens when you don't plan your pregnancy, Miss," I say, both palms against the temples, wondering how on earth I'm going to make this work, then look over at my roommate, like she's supposed to share in my faintheartedness, and she buries her nose in her beer, having read the tips for how to cut the bloat, as if to say *I don't buy it!*

She scratches her head when she puts the glass down. "What if—" she stops, pacing the damp and dingy room, searching for thought, "what if someone forced themselves on her? I mean, what kind of a mother abandons the nest without showing her baby how to fly, escape from predators and integrate with the flock?"

"Noooo. The bitch probably never wanted them. Not that I blame her. Who in the hell would enjoy a jostling around between the two of them as to who's gonna insert the beak into your throat first, and suck the life out of you? They'd be better off dead, or without her," I say, throwing on a long-sleeve shirt, then a cardigan over a turtleneck—layer upon layer to keep warm but it's freezing all the same.

"If I get too close to people," mother whispered in my ear, "they'll guess I had my child killed, have one more reason to hate me."

"You didn't have a choice," I mumbled.

"What would have happened if I had?"

"Mom, I'm not ready for a hike just yet. It's like living in constant fear of having to go under the knife."

"You are not alone."

"But I am, I am, I am…"

It was their smell that woke me up that night but, hard as it was, I managed to fall back asleep, blanket pulled over my head. I saw birds on a leash with cones like lampshades around their necks, parents chewing their own feathers, babies—fat and unfit to take a plunge. I saw mutilated wings, scalps torn back, hearts broken open like doors.

My breathing stopped, and I gasped awake. I knew what I had to do. Didn't hesitate one bit. I stepped out into the night, wrapped them in old newspaper, whose front-page headline read *Dog travels more than 100m to bite its owner after being abandoned*, and laid them next to a dumpster. Then avoided walking past it for days to avoid seeing how they didn't make it.

If their mother lays a new set of eggs, is it ok to get rid of them too? I wondered. To prevent that from happening, I did everything I could think of to keep pigeons off the balcony for good—I had bird spikes affixed, I bought several shiny pinwheels at the dollar store and stuck them in the new flowerpots. I hung everything that twisted and turned on the ceiling, everything noisy that reflected light, and painted the walls orange—it was like nothing had happened. My balcony was pigeon-free and beautiful again.

A few months later, my roommate was having hysterics, raving about a ghost and an uncanny feeling that she was being watched. "Did you know," she asked in bed, "that pigeons mate for life?"

My eyes, not yet open, were two bulbous protrusions on the top of my head. "Shut up!" I cried, "I'm trying to sleep."

In the dead of night, unfamiliar sounds filled the air. Interior doors had been restless for quite some time so we'd keep them from swinging all the way open by leaving them slightly ajar. They were closed when I got up but squeaking just the same.

Walking into the kitchen that opens to the balcony, I turn on the light. There's a painting of an egg hanging on the wall.

Like Falling

We haven't spoken of late. That is, she does all the talking while I'm the silent one, as if silence can somehow protect me. When you decide it's better to scream inside. To sit there like a blunt axe, watch words go by. Maybe because you've seen too many knives, because you aren't rushing to straighten out the cutting edge. Or you didn't know what a knife was until it cut right through your bones with such ease.

I have full access to her cell phone and laptop—think of it as a good sign. She calls it trust building; I don't know what the fuck to call it. She worries my family will be upset if they find out, which is why I haven't told them in the first place. I don't want them to think any less of her. When she says she knows now the grass isn't greener anywhere else, I feel she really means it. I want to trust her again so we recently started *Dr. Lee's Marriage Builders* at home—it has a workbook, a student's book and CDs to go over. I figured, what good are promises without a plan.

Dr. Lee knows best. He knows what's best for me. Dr. Lee knows me better than anyone, suggests I should make a list to ensure she doesn't cheat on me again. So I did. I put the pros and cons down on paper to help me decide whether it was worth going ahead with it to start with, which turned into writing down everything I'd always wanted to say, then, when I felt myself ready, threw it all into her pretty face.

I feel comfortable making lists—short lists, long lists, buying handy little memo pads, magnets and post-its in bulk. Right now, I have a list of priorities, a list of this week's orders, a list of possibilities, probabilities, a list of places to see and people to forget, a bucket list—look into skydiving and such— but unlucky as I am, I'm sure my parachute would open with an error. How do you survive a fall? I wonder. Do you extend your arms and legs into an X to slow it—coz we're just bags of goo, with some bones inside to give us structure, not really made for falls or much of anything—or cross your fingers, repeating *it won't hurt that much, it doesn't hurt at all?*

I stuck today's list on the fridge next to the list of ingredients for mom's walnut cake, then glanced out the window as her car pulled up onto our drive. When I saw her getting near, I drew up a chair to sit at a corner of the table. She grabbed the knob and pushed, hot air rushing into the house, my lungs like old newspapers that you crumple in a sound farewell ritual before throwing them away. The emptiness inside me was physical, as though my heart and liver and all the other organs had been removed.

A salty breeze slid down the hillside to ruffle her hair, dyed a fiery red. She was so beautiful it hurt.

"Transparency!" I yelled out, puffing up my chest to look as big as possible, and she pulled back her chin as if I'd crushed a fly against a wall. "I want to know everything," I lowered my voice not to upset the feng shui in the house. "I am your husband—I have the right to know. I want passwords shared, accounting for finances and time—where, who with, how long, why," I said. Then stopped, bringing my arms and legs in against my body, like a bobsledder, in an attempt to position myself for landing. We watched each other's ribcages go up and down for a while, amazed at how effing loud silence can be.

"No social networking sites," I went on, "no nights apart, no Pilates, no business trips, no inappropriate conversations, no butt comments, no innuendos, no contact with him, *no* contact," I squeezed through the teeth as my hand landed on the table with a thud, pencil rolling across the flat top and off the edge. When I bent over to pick it up, I felt giddy and hit the floor, prayed it was held up by strong wooden supports so I couldn't possibly sink any deeper.

She took a couple of steps toward me. I raised my hand as if to shut her mouth, blinking my eyes as I always do when the tears threaten to return. "No," I yelped before slipping back into silence. "Don't."

137

Movie Night

No spices, no toppings for me—I love my popcorn straight. She loves melted chocolate and black pepper on top. I pour oil into a pot, trying to adjust the amount according to its size, but fail miserably.

"Fuck!"

"Even in the grave all is not lost," my best friend Louise says, entering the kitchen with a joint between her lips. "Lemme do it."

She tosses in a few kernels, then covers the pot to test the oil. The evening is a clump of rock islands on fire— greenish-red hazed in cloud—the sky ragged and broken, like the mountains I left behind.

"I can't do anything right," I say. "Even breathing, my god, you'd think something as easy as that would be impossible to screw up—well, guess what?"

"You mean the diaphragm shit?" she asks before taking a big hit, holding it so long she almost turns blue.

Kernels start jumping up and down, all around, so I add in the rest in an even layer across the bottom of the pot and replace the cover.

"Yeah, like a baby, you know, e-e-e-eeeee"—I push the voice out from my belly.

"Like this," she moves the pot back and forth across the burner, along with her hips, "you need to keep these babies dancing."

The metallic noise overlaps with what sounds like breaking matches. I sway too but her sway's gracious, like that of a gymnast doing a flip, while mine resembles a duck's, desperately trying to force its clumsy body into the splits. After all the kernels have burst open, Louise takes a large bowl from a shelf and fills it with whiteness.

"Serve while still hot."

We eat air, light and fluffy.

"Speaking of which, remember John?" she asks, dipping her fingers into the bowl.

"John who?"

"John Collins, you slut, you fucked him too back in the day!"

I take the knuckle out of my mouth. It looks nasty, as though someone dropped their cigarette (way too many times), burning a hole in the skin. "Give me a blowback, will you?"

She puts the hot end in her mouth, then blows smoke into mine. A fire breaks out in the back of my throat, my tongue smelling like burning rope—a small price to pay for what's to come. I close my eyes for a moment, try to feel it— the fullness of it, the bottomlessness.

"Oh, *that* John!" I exhale. "How could I have forgotten? That was the first time I got laid properly, and the last one for that matter."

"Some use of our husbands, huh? In case of fire," Louise speaks through her nose, "don't open any doors other than the one you need to escape through. And please don't forget to shut it behind you."

"It's like a bank robbery, come to think of it."

"What? Sex?" She raises her ginger brows as we slowly walk toward the bed that hangs suspended in the air like a peach.

"Yeah. I mean, it doesn't have to be a totally unpleasant experience, does it?"

"That Darth Vader voice of his," she adds absent-mindedly. "Mmm hmmm."

"I hate my voice but I'm pretty much stuck with what nature gave me, which isn't much, really." I give a brief shrug of the shoulders. "What the heck, right?"

"I practiced breathing with John once. 'The harder you push,' he said, 'the louder your voice will be.' Wanna try?"

"Now?"

"Yeah. C'mon Thelma, let your hair down for once. Instead of fretting over it, just own the crap out of it. Let's push that baby out, darlin'. Give your Louise one deep strong aaaaaaaaaaa."

Sitting up on the edge of the bed, I spread my legs open and take a deep breath. There's a tingling, stinging sensation down there as the baby's head emerges.

"AAAAAAAAAAAA!!! I FUCKING OWN IT!"

"There you go, hon. It wasn't that hard, was it?"

She pulls down the shutters, plays the movie, and we both crawl in.

"I guess not," I grin ear to ear. "I wish I could love like that—bone-deep, the way a mother loves her child."

"We eat leaves, you and I," Louise chuckles in a happy frenzy, "like moths."

"I'd rather be a grasshopper, hop before you grab it," I say, feeling a kernel shell stuck between my gum and tooth with my tongue. I try to get it out with my fingernail but it won't move. Last time this happened, I brushed, rinsed with water, flossed—nothing! The thing stayed in there for days. "Do you think I could fly like that?"

"Sure you could. It's just that you differ from other insects."

"How's that?" I ask, feeling the kernel way back now. I stick my finger down my throat to scratch it off but it only makes me gag. That's it, no more popcorn for me!

It's soaring hot today. You can smell the starving soil tearing its flesh apart. It's been ages since we last saw tears in the desert sky falling like a loud scream upon the ground, clouds cut open to offer blessings, as if stabbed in the chest by a sacrificial knife. Other than the occasional rumble of thunder in the distance, there's nothing left. Just a silence which perseveres like Sitting Bull.

"Your wings are delicate," Louise says, wiping her forehead with her hand. "If you rub the scales off, you might damage them."

I turn my head toward the window, can't remember the last time I caught the wind, how I held it. I just recall it flying out of my hand—outbreaks of rain, dying out little by little. The mutter of the approaching engine gets louder with each breath I take until it overflows the air. The eerie noises echo through the corridors, in the walls. (If these walls could talk…)

"You sound like you're gonna leave," I say in a small voice, crying silent tears of a mosquito-bitten donkey.

The footsteps have turned steady now, a curtain of shadows lengthening with the setting sun. I'm hoping for a blanket of fog rather than a rain. A fog like that muffles all sounds, and all gets lost within.

"I was thinking we should call him Joshua"—I chew on the inside of my lip, fumbling in the dark for something I think I dropped—"what do you say?"

"Who?"

"Why, the baby! Joshua, my goshua."

The keys jiggle out of the pocket as footsteps draw nearer to the house and wait. Louise grabs a pack of smokes from his nightstand, tears it open and pulls one out with her mouth, then, sliding off the bed, knocks the empty bowl off it.

I tilt my head back. "We didn't finish the movie," I say with a twitch of my nostrils.

"I watched it already," Louise scoffs, peeking through the gaps in the shutters, "I know how it ends. Let me pick next time, ok?" She looks me squarely in the eye when she tells me to keep plummeting downward till I hit the light.

She has a perfectly symmetrical face, her left and right sides like identical twins. Mine's too long, etched with a look of permanent sorrow.

The heat gets sticky and unbearable.

"I'll come for you even from the grave if I have to. Now go get yourself some chocolate, honey, okay? And don't rush—savor every mouthful. It's that hug from the inside. *Okay?*"

"Okay."

I'm doing my best to look suave, but can't shake off that moth I flushed down the toilet. I could have saved it. I should have. And I just watched it go down the drain and be carried away.

Beyond the Ditches

Once darkness falls, Toby and I begin to yawn. Like me, he pretty much gets up when it's light out but can't beat me, really, being an extreme lark and officially the first out of bed.

While the coffee's brewing, I pull the curtain back and look out. The morning is bathed in pale light, the rich, black coal smoke streaming out of the crooked chimneys. There's a brittleness in the sound of air moving through the trees. You can still swim in the lake during the day, though it takes forever for the water to warm up.

As I sip my coffee through a lump of sugar, a gust of wind rattles the window. There's a shout from above, followed by a loud bang. I run up the stairs. I see light coming from Toby's room through a crack in the door, hear squeaking and screeching around the ill-fitted panes.

Stretched out on his bed, his soundless little body gives me nothing to grab onto. The ground beneath me trembles violently, like when a quake roars deeply within the earth, then stills. He's breathing faintly. As if the room filled with smoke, it has become extra hard to take air into his lungs, into mine, even harder to push it out. We sound like the wind that has abruptly and unexpectedly subsided.

***

The next day, Toby's up before me, staring with the agility of a dog, his voice loud and clear like the Sunday church chimes while the buzzing in my ears continues. I help him fold his PJs and put on his fav jersey—Bulls #23. He's thin and flimsy, yet soft to the touch, like silk.

"No!" he cries. "I don't want this one. Take it off, take it off!"

"Ok, ok, which one do you want?"

He points to the bluish-gray sweater with the zip-up front, the one I thought bulky, the one that proved to be flat. Toby's growing and starting to obsess about nice things, and I'm ready to do anything to please him. I put the jersey back—sweaters over jerseys over T-shirts—didn't think I could squeeze any more clothes into his drawers.

Barefoot, I pad down the echoing staircases. Toby comes along, but Toby doesn't walk—Toby sprints and skips and hops. My feet are cold, so cold I can hardly feel the floor beneath them, almost frozen stiff, like after trudging through the snow. I let him slide open the kitchen door before giving him a chair to sit on.

Toby doesn't feel like eating on his own today so I feed him like a toddler, watch milk drip down his chin, specks of cornflakes getting stuck between his teeth. While chewing, he pushes his train set along the tabletop. The tabletop is a piece of solid glass, the kind that doesn't break. His feet can't touch the deep blue tiles. They look as if they're dangling above water.

He pushes the trains over the edge, just for the fun of it, then hits the floor himself, prancing around on all fours like a little show pony. The water is kind. The water won't let him sink. The water is so clear you can see down to the bottom of the lake.

Later, I might take the boat out into the deep where I can dive.

***

The terrible buzzing and ringing starts again, this time louder, much clearer. My chin sinks into my chest, heart freezes in my throat. I signal to Toby, playing in the garden, I'll be right back. Following the sound, I cut across the living room and make for the bathroom, the door sliding shut behind me without my touching the knob.

I fall like rain—enough water to flood the house—then reach up to a high shelf to take down a bottle. "I'll never touch a drop after this, I swear, just one more time," I hiss out through the clenched teeth. "I just need a minute to collect myself."

The heat sears my skin as a flowery taste fills my mouth, lips wavering into a half-smile—I'll be fine, I'll be just fine.

When Noah pushes the door open, the ringing stops. I redden under his gaze, scuttle off like a mouse.

"Tiles and shower walls need cleaning," I say, putting my hands down in a hurry, forcing myself to stand up. "We can do it with a damp cloth. I hate cleaning agents—they stink." When I ask him if he's ok with that, his head gets stuck in an awkward position, like he knows the truth but isn't ready to share it yet. He really makes it hard for me to know what to do.

In the kitchen, I gulp down my coffee. I need to clear up the breakfast things, put the food back in the fridge. (I said I'm fine!)

"Will you help me do the dishes?" I ask. Noah bows his head.

"Alright," he says polishing his glasses, "you wash and I'll wipe."

***

During dinner, the steam breaks through violently, milk boiling over the sides of the pot. I snuff a deep breath and put the knife down before locking the smells inside the walls, fat body waddling off to the porch for an evening cigar. I am blooded and swollen, like a mosquito that slurped up too much red.

"Have you been crying?" Noah asks, forehead creased, blinking like a blackbird perched in a bush of colorful berries, ready to burst from their flesh any moment now. I put my elbows on my knees, tell him I got smoke in my eyes. I don't tell him how much I hate him for being dead. I don't tell him he could have discharged his semen inside my body first. I don't tell him I dream of water pouring out of me, leaving a trail on the floor. I don't tell him I hope there's green somewhere, beyond these muddy fields and burying grounds, past the shadowy silence of decaying trees, behind the dull browns of the mountains—lush green as far as the eye can see, and farther.

Choking on the Bone

Just before my cousin's wedding, Grandpa Yusuf killed Filou. When I asked him if he drew a fork through the fish, he flicked the TV on and, palms forward, moved his bald patch up and down several times. He'd raked out all the bones that appeared rigid, as I told him to, but apparently missed one which stayed lodged in Filou's throat without Baba realizing it. By the end of the day, everything came to a head and he choked.

Filou was terminally ill. A sunken look to the eyes, smelly breath and poor appetite were just a few obvious signs that his days were numbered. And yet, for days I struggled to figure out what I could have done differently to prevent his death. I even tried to strike a deal with a higher power through prayer to bring my cat back, but a friend said I was being silly so I stopped. When I finally came to terms with loss, I set my mind on doing the right thing *this* time. Not bury him in the garden to start with, because if we were to move again, we'd have to leave the remains behind, and it wouldn't be the first time.

Those hazy days of summer were mostly spent cleaning our front yards and houses—wrestling the mattresses outside, beating the dirt out of rugs, running bed covers through the washers before putting them back on—as well as decorating the bedroom where the bride would receive her bridegroom, and the one where the newlyweds would be starting and ending their days from then on. But every evening, however busy I used to keep myself during the day, I expected to see Filou in his usual spots—in Grandpa Yusuf's lap, on the sofa, by the fire—even after my brother brought a new kitten home. Having another animal to care for helped distract me—there's no doubt about it—but I, nevertheless, kept looking for the missing one.

To soothe my conscience, even minimize stress, I decided to plan ahead, that is put the new cat to sleep when the time comes. I'll ask Dr. Ali for one of those shots, which slows their little hearts to a stop—I heard it takes only seconds, they don't feel a thing—and I'll stay with him all the way through, watch his body shut down, pauses between each beat getting longer and longer, the sleep deeper and deeper, until it hurts no more.

At the wedding, the plates were full and abundant in color, whooping guests armed to the teeth with compliments for the bride and groom sitting at a separate table, sneering at each other, polite and aloof, faces twisting gray and cold. And

I kept seeing Filou out of the corner of my eye—raising his nose in the air, sniffing at spiced dumplings, kabab and black caviar from the Caspian Sea—hearing the bride say how after she buried her canary, she would regularly see him in the tree branches above his grave. I should set aside some time for myself each day—a quarter of an hour or so—allow myself to feel my loss. "Go ahead and feel it, girl," she said. "Let it run through you, let your heart ache and tears flow like a river, with the comfort of knowing they will never really be gone, that they'll be stopping by every once in a while just to say howdy."

When the music stopped, the father of the bride inserted the serrated blade into the center of the fish—stabbed it once, stabbed it twice—a glimmer of silver tearing through its delicate flesh. *What a waste*, I thought, winking at her across the room in the *beware of long bones so they don't catch in your throat* way, and she smiled back, then tried to vomit something up in the ladies' room. *Poor Filou*—I finished my drink in one gulp— *it must have been awful for him.*

After the wedding, I decided to buy a knife like that— maybe one for her as well—something that would slice even when the teeth become dull.

When the last guest left, I watched her take off the wedding dress across the town—the one she agreed to wear to avoid more arguments where pushing, slapping and hitting would be involved—hair flowing down her back as she angled her henna-free body away, curling in toward the belly. *I don't want to stain my skin*, she said. Her family placed their hands on their cheeks as if to show they were taking her seriously enough to consider what she was saying, getting all huffy at her complicated ways seconds later.

Just grit your teeth and hang on—I looked daggers at him—*it will be over soon.*

It's Taken a Lot of Pains With Him

Week 1

They'll thrust pins and needles into the doll, and think of pain—back pain, chest pain, stomach pain—all the aches they can call to mind. They don't want to give him all at once, though. They have seven needles for seven weeks.

Nervous in the beginning, they need to think things through before taking an irrevocable step. At first, each of them wants something else—a rope or wire or water—each thinking she stands a better chance of winning the war. They don't agree on everything, of course, but once they decide on a doll, they are ready as they'll ever be.

They want to limit themselves to one color, namely red for power. They don't want energies to become confused and muddled. They will exercise caution, do it slowly and carefully because there's no room for error, because they want to do everything right. They love it when time stretches like canvas pulled over a wooden frame, minutes becoming hours becoming days becoming eternity.

In the first week, they want the pain small in size and amount—all those women he left behind—nothing more than an itch under the waistband or a tingling kind of thing on the eye, a tearful one that makes itself felt, the one that will make him think it can go away if rubbed with his fingernails. But, several days later, everything he wears itches—his hats itch, his sweaters itch, his scarves too—until it gets so bad it's like an itch inside his head. He pulls his skin like a dress, thinks he can almost rip it.

One day, the itch unexpectedly stops and he is in his element again, happy as can be. He is in love, he calls his lover *the man of my dreams*, courageous enough to do something he could never have done with a woman—admit he's gay.

They wrap the doll in gold paper and, digging a hole in the ground, let the Earth cleanse it. They'll give him another gift in a couple days, hope he likes surprises.

Week 2

Lighting a candle, they kneel at the altar they created for the doll. This place is sacred to them, like his life. They unwrap the doll with kid gloves, trying not to tear it like the paper, wet cheeks flushing with joy. They like what they see. They haven't made a doll that represents him. They made a doll that *is* him. The doll is made from two sticks tied in a cross shape. The cross shape is a body. The body is thin, like their past lover, so thin you would see ribs protruding if it were fleshier, arms sticking out as if waving goodbye. They place their hands over the doll and focus their minds before the next needle goes inside.

Limp and relaxed, his lower jaw begins to move involuntary. The corner of his mouth twitches up into his cheek, then falls back. It's weird. He can't smile, let alone laugh out loud. He feels it in his brows, his nose, his ears even—small, unexpected movements he doesn't know how to control—it makes him agitated, he can't think straight.

He's feeling fragile these days, like a butterfly. A thought occurs to him, maybe that's it—it's the butterflies in my stomach.

Week 3

He remembers a superhero blanket he had and loved deeply as a child—the one his mother gave him on the first day of school, the one he used to drag around with him everywhere—and how much he suffered when his father took it away because *you're too old for a blankie*. He remembers a dull pain in his knees long after she left, like the one he feels now. Perhaps she's trying to tell him something, but why now? Besides, it's not just the knees. He's got a slight pain in his side as well, nothing that would require urgent medical assistance, though. He knows he shouldn't worry—*I'm a tough cookie, I'll survive*. Other than that, he feels fine. No, not fine, great, actually. Normal, for the first time in his life. And thankful.

Later in the week, he'll feel a twinge in his back as he bends down. The twinge doesn't go away when he straightens up. The twinge stays.

He's been dreaming a lot lately, mostly of dying a horrible death, with giant ants clawing at his stomach, hundreds of nasty red beings crawling inside him, biting. No, not ants, rats chewing and gnawing at small gaps in his body until the holes are big enough to wriggle through.

Week 4

The shape is covered in a brightly-colored triangle of cloth—he likes all things bright—Spanish moss inside his belly. They like to believe he has a low pain threshold, although they don't really know how much he can stand. Because they never talked about pain with him. Because he hates talking about things that hurt.

Apart from a nagging thing in his stomach, he's ok. He is a free man—that's what matters most. However, his liberated life couldn't have been carried on in the child-centered suburbs, among the people that place a high moral value on marriage, who think raising a family is like trimming a hedge—just a matter of creating a straight line and enviable shapes. When he moved into a bigger apartment in a bigger city, it took time to get used to so much space. Now that he's done it, he's more than ok. The city is undoubtedly noisy and congested, but he doesn't mind—as long as there are no storms with winds sweeping away everything in their path. No one here will ever bother suggesting the sort of lifestyle that would suit him best, or use phrases like *it's for your own good* and the like. He's made an effort to regain lost ground. Now the moon is shining. What more could one wish for?

After they've taken the needle out of his belly, they cup their hands around his head, as if holding a baby in their arms, then kiss him goodnight.

Week 5

They want the pain more specific now. They want to see it, like when you're pulling the meat apart with two forks to look inside.

They'll go all the way—there's no time for waiting. They don't give a fuck about *what goes around comes around* because they've lost everything already so there's nothing left to lose. None of them wants to improve *her* life, really. What all want is to make *his* a living hell.

They take two needles and prick the doll in the head.

He's in the bedroom, making love to his lover when he feels a sudden, sharp neck pain, followed by a stabbing one in the back of the throat, which makes him scream. "I'm sorry," he tells his lover, "I can't." He'll sit long on the edge of the bed, breathe fast and hard, rubbing a washcloth over himself, the pain shifting, spreading from one part of the body to another, expanding. He's got the impression it's playing a trick on him—first it's up, then it's down, then nowhere, finally everywhere. He feels like a melon being cut into sections, knifed to death. When he clenches his arms, his lover pulls them apart.

He'll wake up to his chest exploding, Sunday dawning bright and sunny. He's sure he'll never sleep through the night again.

Week 6

As soon as they poke the last pin in his heart, he'll pass out, lingering in a painful present, tearing his body apart long after he comes round. He swears he can almost feel fingers digging into the flesh between his ribs.

He staggers and slumps onto the floor, like a collapsed corpse. Glassy-eyed and blank-faced, he stares endlessly at his grave. Burial plots are shallow in this city, they say, because there's water everywhere. Dig a few feet down and the grave becomes soggy—his casket will literally float.

They want him in agony by the time he reaches the ER, the one of childbirth that he never got to see, want the doctors to shrug their broad shoulders, *We're terribly sorry, there's nothing we can do to make it go away.* They hope he'll have someone by his side, someone to beg to put him out of his misery. However, they don't want him dead—it would be too easy— they want him alive and suffering.

Shortly after 5 am, the phone rings. It's the police. The neighbors reported hearing a baby cry all night, as well as tiny footsteps on the stairwell. He opens the front door, doesn't see a thing.

When I fall back asleep at long last—he hopes—*I want to dream of dying a peaceful painless death.*

Week 7

He wakes up hugging his knees, defeated, with nothing to hold onto. He dreamed of dying alone. It was downright bone-chilling.

He wanders aimlessly about the apartment all day, feels like an abandoned butterfly garden. No, not the garden, he feels like shit. In the mirror, he is baby-faced and broken-nosed—beyond scary looking, like those dolls with two faces made way back, as if one wasn't creepy enough. He shivers, sinks his teeth into his skin like a dog.

Not strong enough to stand, he crawls to the suitcase his lover left behind. There's a baby inside, not a real baby, but a baby doll. He loves Russian dolls, each unscrewing to reveal a smaller one within. Other than that, he finds dolls eerie as hell—he's heard enough stories of them coming to life to terrorize children and adults alike—and this one is by far the most hair-raising of all, maybe because it looks more human than any other doll he's seen, one of those old raggedy ones with lips that ran dry of all their color, maggots seeping out of their mouths, those smelling like lighter fluid, something you bring back from a trip to South America only to realize too late they are haunted, murdering your neighbors in their sleep, unspeakable evil coming to anyone who hears their terrifying cackle.

He pictures his past lover as a sinister little boy, playing with dolls in a dilapidated house with a leaky roof. That would have left a mark, though, and his skin is so perfect—not a blemish on it. He doesn't know the story behind the doll or why it is in his apartment, but obviously he can't throw it in the trash. He thinks it disrespectful so he washes it clean, lets it dry on the clothesline. When he puts her dress back on, he will make sure he finds her an appropriate place—somewhere nice, somewhere close to him. There's a gap between his mattress and headboard. Maybe there.

He can hardly keep his eyes open. He is so tired he could sleep for a week.

All the women he left behind look up at the stars in the night sky one last time before sinking into slumber with their eyes wide open. They have daggers too and instructions on how to use them, but it has been decided that it's enough.

Now that the pain has subsided to a dull ache, we'll let him rest—hopeless and all alone.

Cutting

To be frank, it took me forever to find something that worked. I tried quitting so many times but it's easier said than done. I gave up smoking much faster.

Personally, it never bothered me. It seemed to have bothered everyone else, though, because, over the years, I'd been regularly given advice on how to stop. Interestingly, I wasn't always aware of what I was doing. I could be busy doing one thing, then, before you know it, my finger's in my mouth.

The shrink next door had a name for it. *A body-focused repetitive disorder*, he stated one day, patting his orderly hair, after which he cleaned his apartment, loaded the gun—a .357 revolver he had for protection—and pulled the trigger. I thought of the path of the bullet, the sound it made ripping through his skull. Google was convinced I was focused on high performance and excellence, which often come at severe cost, or that I was just idle, suggesting chewing gum so my mouth had a job. The kids at school laughed. *It's like sweating*—daddy gagged and coughed, choking on his own spit—*like sweating in a most unladylike manner.* Then took the necessary steps to break me from the habit—gloves at night, nail polish so foul it made me want to puke, all possible nail files he would find on the market so I could neatly trim them, hoping there's less temptation to bite when they are smooth. Ma mostly kept silent. He'd take it out on her, pulling back as if before the point of a knife, or beer cans and rabbits with his shooting buddies, she on small objects around her. I was doing it on nails. Nails were always there, letting me form my own opinion about it.

I remember one drizzly November evening when daddy came home drunk as a skunk, dragged ma out of bed and made her watch him climb on top of me and cut my nails so short I felt naked. Later that night, I finished them off swiftly and without mercy, biting them up past the nail bed. Before dropping my head back against the pillow, I put a tight band-aid around them so my skin wouldn't move, which was just about the only thing that made my fingers hurt less. I was fine in the morning. Mornings are gentle and forgetful.

In high school, I mull over how my nails will change with age, how they'll start growing more slowly, become dull and thick, how I'll want to grow them back but won't be able to. So I try hard do to something about it, but I'm a natural-born quitter.

"We need to keep your hands and mouth busy," my biology teacher says, unzipping his pants, "find you something to fiddle with: a stress ball, a worry stone"—he begins to stroke—"a pen to click." Then grabs me by the neck to pull me forward. I yelp like a puppy when I hit the floor.

I thought it would be easier when I started going steady with this guy I met at a job fair because every time he'd see my fingers in my mouth, he'd tell me to stop.

"That's disgusting," he would say turning on the warm water faucet, letting his hands get wet all over. "Nails are filthy. When I think of all those bacteria that end up in your mouth…"

He dispenses liquid soap onto his skin and rubs his hands together, scrubbing between fingers and washing around his wrists and under his nails, as if getting ready for the operating room.

"What if they get infected? Think of warts and herpes, Jesus, don't you hate it?"

"I do," I say, drawing deep unsteady breaths, like a little girl unable to express herself without fear of criticism.

He turns off the faucet with the same towel he dried his hands with. "And?"

"And what?" I snap. "I don't pick my nose. I don't drink. I'm a nail biter! Sue me!"

When I think about him, I think about his skin—flat and tight like a dead man's—and hand sanitizers, bio-detergents and antibacterial bar soaps he bought in bulk.

"These will protect your nails from dirt," he'd say, pointing to the gloves he used for digging or washing, "stop harsh cleaning agents from damaging your skin. And we don't want that, do we? These can make your fingernails heal, repair themselves."

I move in a jerky kind of way, transferring my weight from one foot to another, like they do in foxtrot, to avoid stepping on his carpets. Until one day, I ran out the door in my house clothes, jumped into a cab and went back to scratching the mud under my fingernails with my teeth.

Then Sam came along. We hit if off right away. After dating for just two weeks, I moved in with him.

"Are you hungry?" he asks in a slow lazy tone, throwing his head back, lips ready to break into a smile.

"Maybe," I say, pressing my lips with a slight frown. "What's it to you?"

"I bet you get a real kick out of it."

This is when the shame would kick in. But not this time. Not with Sam. So I tell him. "It feels fucking amazing! At times I go so far that my fingers bleed and I cringe in pain, which clearly doesn't bother me. I love sucking my blood— simple as that."

Sam opens the window, light breeze clutching at the curtains, then goes on to make a fresh pot of coffee, says this one's cold. The rooftops glisten in the rain, thick clouds thinning out. You can see pieces of the blue sky already. The city will have such a clean smell all day long.

"Do you think I should keep them short, like real short? I figure, if there's not enough nail to grab, it won't feel as good."

He furrows his nicely defined brows—"It seems easier to please others, doesn't it?"

I stare hard at my fingernails. Maybe I should start painting them. "You'll be surprised, but I actually like them long."

"Good," he says, wrapping himself around me, his hands sure and subtle against my skin.

And just like that, I've stopped cutting my nails. This is how I heal.

Earth-shattering (The Life and Death of Mr. Rupert)

Breathe, I told myself, crouched inside a pit, waiting for my eyes to adjust to the dark, then shivered again after stepping on dry crunchy leaves. I came down to earth with a bump when I realized the pit was real, that I wasn't dreaming. It smelled bad and I felt dirty. Not sure how to explain it...somehow the earth appeared unearthly. I didn't like it, not one little bit. I felt it underneath alright, though it was as if I didn't, as if it had slipped from under my feet and I dangled helplessly from a cliff, trying not to look down.

Taking a few steps in all directions to get at least a faint idea of the hole size, my pupils opened up, allowing my eyes to collect whatever light there was. Obviously, it was high enough for me to stand in, a bit more than the width of my outstretched arms. I'd say about 6 feet by 6 feet. Also, it contained no personal possessions or anything else that would help me figure out where I was. It was like a mystery object I needed to guess—but how?

Much of my memory was gone as well, the whole thing reminding me of limbo where nothing ever happens and nothing ever changes, which makes it hard to know what to do, let alone what to expect. So, just like that, I found myself waiting for something to happen first.

For a while, I pictured myself lying in a pool of sunlight warming my withered bones, that is after I saw my breath in the air, which was very discouraging, to say the least. I didn't want *this*, whatever it might be, *this* that made me feel like I had something stuck in my throat, *this* that made me think *dieu est mort, heaven is empty*.

My intonation had been unmistakably genteel, voice clear, somewhat authoritative, sure of itself— I knew that much. Now the pins and needles sensation around the mouth and lips wouldn't let go. Honesty, if I had a chance to talk to someone, they wouldn't have the slightest idea what I was saying as my speech would be slurred and barely comprehensible. My hips, feet and arms hurt too, a constant dull pain I was feeling, a reminder that the muscles, tendons and ligaments had been immobile for quite some time.

Think! I yelled at myself, eyes swimming in and out of focus, then straightened my legs until I was standing upright. Think hard! How did you get here? You slipped and fell?

Someone pushed you? Maybe I suffered a blow to the head, which would make sense, and in case I hit it, how do I know it's nothing serious?

Sweat streamed from my armpits, heart pounding harder against my ribs. I was losing it and in dire need of some rational thinking to indulge reminiscing, encourage it, which was a critical step in the right direction, that is if I was to stand any chance of getting myself back up. But, to start the ball rolling, I had to calm down first. I inhaled through the nose, took in a lot of air until my lungs felt full, held it there for a few seconds, released, breathed in, breathed out, repeated. When my breathing became steady, I knew the time was right. Step by step, I went back in time in an attempt to recollect things from different time sequences, first remembering the most distant events and faces, though each new period of time was becoming more difficult to recall to memory. I seemed to have a distorted sense of time passing. Some people were there, then they weren't. Some things made sense, others didn't. Without doubt I needed more information to create a whole picture, but how do I obtain it?

It was like using flashcards to engage active recall, mine, however, being full of holes, incomplete and therefore hard to navigate, bearing questions on one side and no answers on the other. It felt like looking through an old photo album.

The pictures surfaced, at least some did, although it would sure as hell help if there were names and dates underneath.

I saw lights flashing, heard metal bending and crashing and crunching. I remembered a woman washing her hair—abundant and pale brown—way back, cool breeze drifting through the window, someone in the garage, four bikes driving around, a freight truck accelerating, snapping and grinding as his front tires drove over me, insides cracking when his back tires did the same. People come rushing, *oh my god, he's alive.* I can't feel my fingers, can't see my arm, can't see other cyclists. I see my chest rising and falling—and yet I can't take a breath—tubes running into my nose, into my mouth, masked faces hovering over me, don't see a thing. *It's god's will now.*

His fingers moved. "Mr. Rupert, can you hear me? Blink if you can hear me."

I remember the breathing tube removed, and foul smells—catheter bags, toting a colostomy bag. *He'll need a walker. He walks.* "You walk again, Mr. Rupert, it's all up to you now."

I stare at my reflection in a brightly-lit bathroom. I don't know this man, this grown-up man and the time he's in. It's stone cold. Nothing stirs, either in the air or in the bosom. I fall into the never-ending pit of darkness. Can't tell whether I'm breathing or not.

I have a memory like a sieve, forget what I'm doing here, what I'm supposed to do. I write a diary not to forget things, countless entries filled with prosaic happenings—Mr. Rupert woke up at 6 am today/ watched his cat wash herself after breakfast/ went to work (yes, Mr. Rupert has a real job now)/ filled in forms/ listened to the keys jingling, elevator doors dinging, vacuums whirring/ caught the 5 o'clock bus (thinks driving a real chore)/ peeked at college kids, guessing who's gonna end up a nervous wreck and who a pretentious ass/ imagined his neighbors talking behind his back/ fed the cat/ didn't eat his dinner/ did listen to voicemails (although too much excitement before bedtime can make it hard to fall asleep)—no messages.

The memories were becoming jumbled. I began having an irregular heartbeat once again. It struck me that unless I have a photographic memory, I'd most likely forget half of what I remembered. I needed to control my thoughts, but how do I do that when I'm not able to concentrate on one thing for more than a couple minutes? As time went by, I was less sure how to dig myself out since every new explanation of how I got there seemed less believable than the previous one. In the end, it mattered little. The only thing I knew for certain was I wanted out. The cold from the frozen soil below would deep-freeze the warmest of hearts. Think!

I'm hearing voices, seeing things—disturbing things, things I don't want to see. Old memories have faded, new memories have replaced them.

I remember taking interest in a girl whose father was a pastor, feel warmth rushing back into my fingers, remember how it felt. I see my face stuck in a screaming position with no sound coming out—another incomplete flashcard, another hole in the wall.

I smell burnt wood. There's a fire burning somewhere. She invited me to church one evening, dry and crisp like today, and I was thinking *this will be easy* but inside was so fired up— throaty coughs, tongues talking, over the top, like coaches excited about winning—and I never liked big crowds and big games. But the pastor had fire in his eyes so I went back. My constant unrest drove me to seek after God because I knew only the Lord could give me what my soul longed for. I prayed, read the Bible, did good things, still being tormented within. After months of searching for answers, I realized there were things that I needed to repent of, people I needed to turn away from. When I did, God started speaking to me. It was like using a wet towel to smother the fire. I was saved.

I believe I jumped into the hole and when it was time to leave, I couldn't. As if instead of a tree root or a rock, I was grabbing onto my arms and legs to stop myself from coming up to the surface. I felt a throbbing chest pain—maybe I fractured a rib when I fell. I rubbed my unshaven cheeks, coughed a little, heard rattling and wheezing at every breath— maybe I have lung cancer.

It crossed my mind that not having a shovel might be a good thing as digging would only make the pit deeper. There's no way I could build a ladder to climb up either, so I picked up a dirt clod and flung it toward the opening, hoped someone would see it, hear it. Being in a cemetery would be a promising sign, however morbid it sounded, because people die all the time, they need to be buried, gravediggers hurling earth into the pit. If this was a grave, I wondered what it looked like. I love those ancient neglected ones that nobody ever visits, a rusty iron cross glowing on a stone wall.

God took her from me, I knew that. Froze her to death—a bloody-minded, murderous psychopath! I saw my loved ones slipping from my grasp and behind the horizon, watched my life collapse and come tumbling down on me like a huge mountain, remembered how it felt. All of a sudden I realized the hole looked strangely familiar. I couldn't be more certain I'd been there before, or that it was no different from all the others I'd dug. It called out to me. There was this husky whisper at the bottom of it saying *come on down, you'll like it here*, and I did. Walking down the narrow roads, I squinted into the darkness, buried myself beneath a pit of earth so deep no one has been able to find me. I feel good here. And it smells just fine.

What I Love About My Mother Is She's Dead

It's not like I don't want to love my mother. It's just that I don't know how. I think I hate her too much to love her. What's there to love? She never washed herself and smelled of rotten flesh and piss. Told me I was evil, that I'd burn in hell for not taking better care of her. And she was a mess, accumulating junk by the piles. The whole house was, with pizza boxes and beer cans all over. I remember when she smashed all the mirrors, when she said she was fat and ugly. She was right.

"I need my garbage!" mother would snap at me if I dared to throw something out. She'd call 911 and cry into the phone receiver that I was on the cusp of a breakdown and she was worried I might hurt myself.

"My poor sick baby," she'd say in an undertone, looking over her shoulder at me being tied up, eyes cutting deeper than any knife.

The crazy bitch told the police once we were black. Father wrestled the telephone from her hand, threw it over the fence and onto our neighbor's driveway. I often dream of a female officer holding a gun to his forehead, screaming to know if he was armed.

On a sticky summer day, father threw away a bunch of her stuff. She flipped and threw him out. When he came back after a month, he packed his shit and left without uttering a word. Her biggest regret was that she didn't get a chance to spit in his eye.

I don't have a single photo of mother. Sometimes I close my eyes and try to picture her—the way her hair fell over her face, the sound of her footsteps. Sometimes I think I see us wrap our arms around each other and yell *snuggles!* Sometimes I hear her tell me I'm pretty.

No one ever told me I was pretty. I wanted to become love and threw my arms around men's necks, wishing they'd believe I was, trying to fool them into saying it. If only someone would bury their head in my lap and ask *where did I go wrong?*

They jab the steak with a fork over the Super Bowl, "Can we do this another time?"

I take a long drag on my cigarette, fingers stained yellow from years of smoking, push out smoke rings with a small jut of my jaw. "Sure, baby," I simper, unable to sit still, "whenever you say."

I have been reading self-help books lately—*All About Me*, *All About Love* and *All About My Mother* kind of crap—hoping I could love her someday.

When she passed, I had a grab bar installed in the shower but my legs cracked off like a branch and I fell. Then I trashed everything till there was nothing left—nothing but ugly, dirty walls. I feared mother would suddenly jump out of the shadows, start kicking me and barking, but she just sat there in the back of my throat like a fish bone.

I am an island. I don't need nobody. I had a dog a while back but couldn't stand the noise so I took him by the collar and dragged him out—out of my bed, out of the house, out of the city.

It's just me and the boxes now, empty boxes I can't howl down.

Come With Me If You Want to Live

Xena is a robot, I thought. She must be because that's what robots do. That's what a robot would do. I mean, how can you trust something that can't look you in the eye, to start with?

There were times when she was aware of herself, Xena the robot, asking the voices in her head to shut up, begging me to forgive her. Times when she was normal. I think it depended on when she took her medicine.

Robots don't know they are robots so you can't be mad at them for doing stupid things or failing to meet your expectations. Xena is ill and it's not her fault. It's nobody's fault. I tried to remember that next time she tried to hurt me.

Oddly enough, I had always known robots would eventually take over, making our lives a grueling and dangerous journey, until we lose the right to decide our own future. Actually, my greatest fear wasn't that robots might come for our lives. It was that they had already become our bosses.

***

There's nothing like being served by someone who seems to genuinely want to be serving. At least, that's what it looked like in the beginning, but that changed. Xena changed, and so did my life. The first thing I lost was my social life. I stopped seeing my friends, always racing to meet her metrics, tethered to her needs like a monkey chained to a stake beside the waterhole.

Then she began stealing my makeup, trying on my shoes—so not cool! I swear to god there were times when I thought she was doing it on purpose, for attention—walking into my room to rip out pages from my books, calling me at work, embarrassing me in front of the girls—but when she started taking my dirty clothes to wear, I knew there was more to it than a mood swing. It turned out she was mentally ill, and I began to hate her for it. And it's not only the diagnosis, don't know, we simply never connected and my parents didn't make it any easier.

When we were little, she tried to push me down the stairs. Mom gave her my ice cream, let her bury her face in her chest. She said Xena was going to be alright, everything was going to be alright.

Their attitude didn't change much when we hit puberty. Dad didn't want it to change.

"Don't you see she gets picked on at school?" he said, bottles rattling as he stacked the beer crates, and she pulled a face at me behind mom's back, then took her plate over to another table. It suddenly crossed my mind that she might be an advanced robot because most robots I'd known sucked at comedy, but the very next moment she proved me wrong, going down to the basement in sullen silence as if to say *I don't want your fucking dessert, leave me alone!*

A few years later, she stalked a popular kid at school— I never told mom—lying about him liking her and when he said he didn't, she came to the conclusion it was because he was bisexual, though he wasn't and everybody knew he wasn't. In the end, she made herself look like a frigging clown. That's when things started getting really heavy.

The worst was the *but she's family*. For me, being linked to someone by blood doesn't automatically mean you have to like them. Xena is a schitzo robot. By the time we get her fixed, I thought once, many times, human civilization will come to an end.

My then-boyfriend didn't think I needed to feel sorry. "Those feelings you have are natural," he said, "*she* is unnatural." He even suggested I should file a police report next time she gets physical with me. The worst thing was knowing he was right. Trouble was, the police would have to come over and mom was home 24/7—she would kill me.

My parents weren't very educated. They were embarrassed to file for disability for her to maybe even out some expenses, convinced her condition was the devil's work, that she was possessed, calling in a priest to drive out evil spirits and wash her like a cat, because *to be virtuous is to be physically clean.* I'd ball up my fists before entering the house, sweat dripping down the sides of my head at the thought of the ordeal ahead.

"If you feel like you need a break," mom said on one occasion, "you can hit pause and punch out." The whole thing drained me to the point where I was feeling like a robot myself but, regardless, I stayed.

***

Xena hooked the bucket onto the rope and lowered herself down. Fearful of our well becoming contaminated, she decided to check all the waterways that silted up. In her precarious state, she had bridges to cross, paths to clear.

"I want to go deeper down," she said before she set off, "see what's inside," and we let her because otherwise she would have pressed the *I'll give them hell* button, then repeat, because the whole house was spick and span by the time she came back, which would have been less probable if she had been around. Xena never helps with the housework anyway.

182

She rather monitors the progress, tells you how quickly she would do the vacuuming herself, or *it sure looks good to see a clean floor space—you missed a spot.*

I knew all along what she'd say when she got back. I called it fake empathy, her sounding chipper and being like *oh, I'm so sorry I couldn't help.*

While setting the table, she went so hungry her stomach hurt. Mine tightened at the sight of her hands caked in heavy clods of wet earth. Xena is a dirty robot, I thought, feeling like a sponge full of unshed tears, sponging her down on the bathmat as she confided that she found a long canal where all the dead bodies had been thrown. When we sat down to lunch, she said we better eat indoors, "it smells like rot here."

***

Every evening right before bed, I had a feeling if I stretched the muscles I had used during the day and allowed my breathing to return to normal, I would stand a chance of falling asleep faster, although nights didn't give me much comfort either. It felt like relaxing on inflatable rubber tubes, pool packed to the brim, with very little space to float around.

Once, she startled me awake in the gray half-light of dawn to give me a kiss on the lips. That's when I knew I'd get my life back on track only when she dies.

"You're not stopping!" I cried, leaping out of bed like the fish out of the water, "You're fucking never stopping," and she burst into laughter, said, "I'm sorry, I haven't had much to smile about lately." It was like leaving the house and just running, not stopping for anything for hours, just running, except I always ran screaming, with a child in my arms.

I don't ever want to have kids, I kept telling myself. I don't ever want to have kids.

***

My stomach heaved, compressing muscles deep into my ribcage, a stabbing pain in the back of my throat making it impossible to articulate a sound, when I heard Xena died. I had moved out several years before, waited till the time was ripe to tell my parents I failed some exams, that I had my own life to lead, my own baby to raise. I said I'd visit everyone, find the time to make the rounds. Keeping his arms straight, dad raised them as high as he could, then clenched his hands above his head. He said Xena was going to be alright, everything was going to be alright. Mom thought less forceful followers may find it impossible to challenge the leader.

Me, I convinced myself I wouldn't allow myself to feel too much pain if this was to happen but at some point realized how cruel it sounded and decided it had to hurt some. She's your sister after all. It has to hurt some. I thought it would be more of a vague, if not dull, feeling, though, like when you strain a muscle working out in the yard, causing mild physical discomfort, displeasure, nothing that painkillers and time couldn't relieve. And yet, those were the groans of a woman in labor, when your flesh is red and covered in sores—so fucking hard to survive. Xena the robot is dead and it's my fault, I thought. It's all my fault.

As time went by, the pain turned into a fluttering sensation in my stomach, almost like when I was expecting and the baby moved in the same location a few times.

***

I knew it could be heritable, her condition, but still, after Xena was gone, I needed to feel something alive inside of me. The doctor suggested a C-section this time because of a high-risk pregnancy, and I said no—I want to see with my own eyes all the pain I'll be going through.

"South Korean women are quiet during childbirth," the midwife spoke in whisper, stroking my restless belly, brittle wafer dissolving against the roof of her mouth, "you don't want your family to be ashamed of you, do you?" I threw my head back screaming at the top of my lungs the way my robot Xena and I did, pretending to be helicopter rotor blades spinning at full speed, skirts swirling around our legs as if dancing. We thought they could hear us on the Moon.

She Hummed an Air

On a nearly empty night train, you listen to the rhythm of the wheels gripping the railroad track to pass the time on your commute when something makes you turn and you see them—creeps and weirdos you were warned away from, tiptoeing everywhere like trespassers. Mother drilled it into you not to smile at strangers, you should know better, but you feel it just the same—a tingliness in your knees, like when the weather's changing. It's like you have a second pair of eyes on the back of your head, their stare boring into you as you gaze into space, cutting through you like a hot knife through butter. Don't turn around—you curl your fingers into a fist—no matter what, don't turn around!

You hear your bones creaking as time stretches like a spider's web. It feels like walking between subway cars, air humming deep tunes like jumbo bass fiddles. You watch a flat piece of glass slide open, see other girls making their way up the stairs, think of them holding onto the handrail, lowering their heels down before rising up onto their toes to make sure no one is following them. You hear loud screams from unexpected directions as the doors slide shut.

They hear them too, standing stiffly, listen to them hard, like dolls waiting to be picked up and repositioned. Beside themselves, they rush to the elevator that's just another slow train, hundreds of feet below sea level—it will never reach the surface, never see the light. Once they are outside, in the open air, they laugh so much they almost cry. They think, it's ok now, now that I don't feel their fingers brushing mine, sending my pulse racing, now that I see other people, and cars, so many cars and motorbikes spitting sparks like an open fire—raging, roaring, spreading. My bus will be here any minute now, it's ok, they comfort themselves, sweat dripping down their chests, until a face shadowed with sorrow comes up to them and confides it lost its way in the dark, doesn't know the city. *Could you tell me how to get to...*and *would you mind showing me the way*, the face asks, *I didn't mean to startle you, I feel so lost.*

Air swelling inside them, around them, they'll remember a movie in which a girl dies from a single knife wound, but *it won't happen to me, he looks decent—he wouldn't hurt a fly.* They'll think about death after they've survived all their mistakes. They take a deep breath. When they let it out, the stranger's lips part in a straight smile.

On a nearly empty night train, I plant my two feet back on solid ground, take the seat opposite a pensive woman, chin propped in her hands. I don't think they can see me. No one can see you if you're looking down, like when your eyes are hidden behind sunglasses. The train switches over to another track, the clickety-clack noise as safe as a lullaby. When it grinds to a halt, I ease my way toward the door. All that exists is my breath.

At Christmas We Don't Trim the Tree, My Neighbor and I

*O*uch is all I got from my asshole neighbor, shears in his hands, sharp blades snipping through hard, woody stems, a lame and tired *ouch* after I confided that I cut my thigh with a hedge trimmer. I cut it pretty good, thought I'd put a band-aid on it and see what happens, "but when the fat started spilling out, I fucking shit myself—eight stitches, man!"

Someone said it's the property, the reason why I often hurt myself *unintentionally*, as the previous owner died here—it must be haunted—but I love it here and can't be bothered with superstition. It brings bad luck anyway. It's a beautiful and practical house, although it wasn't always like that. When I bought it a few years ago, it looked like a neglected hedge—it needed rejuvenating—and it took a lot of money and nerves to make it livable again. Now that everything is where it's supposed to be, I just ensure it looks its best by regularly scrubbing it clean and cutting down the hedge to a manageable height and width.

On the weekends, I'm usually in the garage out front, with my tools, the kind of tools that can hurt you real bad if you use them the wrong way or aren't careful, but without them I am nothing short of stranded. Last year, I smashed my finger with a hammer while setting some shelves, hit it so hard it split the end of my thumb. It was horrible, every nerve in my body hurt, and at the Urgent Care they were like *oh, it's you again.*

I have a rental as well, in the backyard. The last tenants, a noisy family of six, moved out after a year, owing three months, leaving all their stuff there—their wreaths, stockings, string lights too—and I spent days cleaning the house from top to bottom after I got the furniture out. They broke four doors, cracked the inside of the fridge, put food in floor vents—it's been a nightmare. Anyway, the other day I was going to trim the out-of-control shrubbery around that house but trimmed my thigh instead. My arms began to tire from holding the hedge trimmer that kept running several seconds after I turned it off, slicing through my pants and into my leg.

I knew I shouldn't have let them in the moment I heard those screaming brats, not to mention the wife's annoying and disruptive laughter, but didn't want to sound like a jerk. Besides, I thought it was only temporary.

Someone told me a way to get people out when they don't want to leave—a guy I worked with at a brick factory—you just go there and take the front door off the house. At first they'll be like *whaaaaat*, but when you tell them you need it on another house where they are paying the rent, they ask no more. Trouble is, my last tenant was ex Black Ops, I wouldn't fuck with him.

I rarely talk but when I do, I barely pause for breath. "Shears are better," I tell my neighbor scanning his hedge—bald in patches like his beard, in desperate need of filling out, like him—"it's work but no fingers get in the blades, or so I've heard." Then I say I feel shitty, and whenever I feel shitty or something happens that makes me want to die, I do stuff to take my mind off it—hop on my bike or call someone, though I'm often not sure who to call. Or I just stay in the garage, "and now with this leg—"

He's weird, my neighbor. Everyone would say something, something nice, something human, like *tea, cats and movies*, and he just stares in horror as if unsure how to trim the overgrown hedge without killing it.

The Worlds That Never Were

Everything she said was true. I would never get to graduate, never go to college, have kids—the list of nevers goes on and on. I'd expected something familiar, though, like a metallic taste of blood in your mouth after biting the inside of your cheek. And yet, it was nothing you can put a name to. It happened suddenly, in our home at the birthday party celebrating my coming of age, with lots of laughs and booze, when I looked big and important, when I thought I'd look bigger holding my dad's gun, waving it around, until I put it to my temple and Nina screamed *stop, it's not funny anymore, stop right now!* So I did—just didn't know it was loaded. Mouth wide open, I fell facedown on the floor of my parents' bedroom. I felt nothing, and felt it so completely.

***

The woman standing by a desk, engrossed in the paper, told us to make ourselves at home, she'd be with us in a moment. I was curious as to what she could be reading but clearly there was no way of finding it out so I had to be patient, like the rest.

The room was dimly lit and tastelessly furnished—a mass of color, crammed with a bunch of stuff I thought odd or hopelessly outdated—a heart-shaped carpet, two narrow desks in the middle and an oversized cabinet with a poster of a rooster picking at grain in the back, a rotary dial phone on a cheap coffee table next to it. In plates all around were stones, gems and smoldering joss sticks. And then there were noises coming from behind the walls, skittering sounds, buzzes and squeaks—unexpected and persistent. I'd lived long enough with radiator heat to know how loud pipes can be or an unbalanced washer or a window that succumbed to time. It wasn't that. The shrubs around the house were high enough to protect it from the street noise, so it wasn't that either. It was more like when there's something living in the house that's not part of the family or among the living.

"Money first," the woman turned to us, opening a small metal box for us to insert 7,000 drachmas. "The session lasts half an hour," she added and we nodded silently.

"Blessed among women!" she raised her voice confidently after she put away the box, her smile revealing a row of strong healthy teeth you see in people with obligatory health care. "Who is the palm reading for?"

"Him!" Nina said loudly to get her attention, pushing me forward.

The noises faded away, which left me with a sense of unease. I felt exposed, naked, standing there all alone. I knew the whole thing would be like posing for a painting the woman would give a distinct shape to, afraid, though, that when she turns the canvas around I won't like what I see.

"It's a birthday gift."

I think she thinks I want to impress them. She thinks I think it's all a scam.

"When is your birthday?"

"In a couple months, then he's going to college," Nina went on. "He's the smart one."

"That's a nice gift," the woman pointed to the chairs.

I sat at one desk, she at the other, across from me, my three girlfriends took their seats against the wall, to my right.

"Do you know anything about palmistry?" the woman asked, looking me in the eye, the girls snickering at what seemed science fiction to all of us. Obviously, I couldn't tell her that the idea scared me to death. I hesitated, like when you're standing under the eaves, knowing you have to get going, hunching your shoulders against the rain.

"I'm not sure...Yes, I think I do...Yes," I said feebly, feeling my heart racing in my stomach.

She tells me to hold out my hands. "The left one is what you're born with, the right your own story. Something tells me you're interested in the latter."

Everyone nods in agreement.

The woman puts on her green-rimmed glasses, cups my hand and watches it long, as if peering into a house, nose pressed against the glass. She studies the shape of my hand, touches the lines and mounds in the palm. Gently. Carefully. As if not to disturb or miss something. Then rises to her feet and tilts her head. To the left. To the right. Like the way you see things differently depending on where you stand.

Resuming her seat, she squeezes my wrist as though to stop the bleeding, then pinches the fleshy bit below my fingers.

"Your heart is easily broken," she says after a pause. "On the bright side," her keen eyes light up like a cat's, "you are a good secret-keeper, which is why women love you."

I stretch my mouth politely, the girls giggling like there's a male stripper with six-pack abs right in front of them—loyal, sweet and eager to please.

"Were you ever hospitalized?"

"No."

"Injured?"

I shake my head, twisting in my seat.

"There's an empty house, a lot of sadness. Did you have some emotional trauma?"

I check the clock. Exhale sharply.

"Plenty of changes in life from external forces," she says with awkward sympathy. "Many of the things that happened to you were out of your control...I see a woman—hair nicely done, purse slung over her shoulder—hear the fall of dropping water."

Silence reigns between us for a while. I check her out like someone you want to get to know—the length of her hair, the color of her skin, shape of her eyes. She looks mundane, earthly, has one of those faces you're sure you've seen before but don't know where. I expected her to look different. Don't know what I expected, really. Someone old and ugly. A witch breaking bones with her bare hands, head tied up in a black scarf.

The woman put my hand down, folded her thin fingers into a cross and screwed her face into an expression of pain.

"Your mom died recently, didn't she?"

"How do you know?" I asked in a flat voice. Then again, I thought the whole world knew and if they didn't, they should, including her. I opened and closed my mouth a few times before anything came out, as if struggling to climb out of a ditch.

"Yes," I swallowed, staring vaguely at her, feeling sweat dribbling down my arm, forming a puddle in the palm of my hand.

All of a sudden, the whole place erupted in a cacophony of hoots, cackles and wails, like when you give instruments to two-year-olds and expect them to play Mozart. The landscape and people changed, the rivers turned red, the sky paled. We grew edgy, started digging deep into things that weren't there. Mom was never the same when we moved to Serbia. We had to drag words out of her but it felt odd, like trying to take a cat for a walk. She would say things like *it's too crowded, I can hardly move,* even when there was no one but us around. When all you need is a long silence, but can't concentrate because of a drip, drip, drip, the plink-plink sound of a dripping water faucet you hear all the time. Dad didn't come along. He said *they'll take me for a coward if I leave.* Mom took him for a coward for staying. When he joined us, much later, he was like a silencer. The sound was missing, though it hurt just the same.

Before the war, our life in Bosnia was small and unburdened. What I loved about my parents was they never allowed their mood to affect their relationship with my sister and me. And it was all about rituals and harmony, car rides and board games, finding small ways to show we cared for one another. Mom was a classy lady with a distinct sense of style, rather unconventional for such a small town, besides being a woman of her word, reliable and consistent—*a masterpiece of low-keyed eloquence,* as dad used to say. It's true. She didn't talk much but had a way with words, knew exactly how to choose the right ones. He, on the other hand, was a motormouth, always in a joking, upbeat mood, and although he was often away on business, that didn't stop him from being the best dad in the world. Most importantly, he kept his promises and obligations. It wasn't in his nature to give up or back out. We loved him for it.

"Imagine a perfect vase—like this one," I said, eyes on the one on her desk, with four bamboo sticks.

I turn my head sharply, feel a pinching pain in my neck, toward the base of the skull.

"Then it falls down. At one corner, a large chunk has been knocked out, leaving a nasty, jagged edge."

I leap to my feet. Can't seem to turn my head to either side without an unpleasant physical feeling. My teeth chatter, muscles tense up.

"Mom loved water. She was like an otter—swam well and ate fish all the time.

I drop into another chair, hoping the aches would stop there.

"I remember dad saying how she pushed herself into a tub of hot water, as if she wanted to stay there...It wasn't water after all."

The corners of my mouth are cracked and sore, so I ask for water. The woman pours it from the pitcher until it touches the rim of the glass. I spill some on the desk, my shirt, pants, feel it down my chest, put the glass down, inhale.

"Dad was an idealist. He refused to see bad in people, liked to believe they are genuinely good—before the war got the better of him. As time dragged on, he got worse. After mom's death, he was but a distant reminder of grandeur. Any attempt to bring him back to life equaled stitching a seam with wrong sides together."

I force words into my mouth but the taste of them only makes me nauseous.

"It's me who found her—stark naked, hanging from the chandelier, pink tongue sticking out. I felt like a dull knife—couldn't cut her down—and when I did, it was too late. When dad came home, he flung himself down with a groan, like someone plunged a blade into his chest."

The woman cleared her throat loudly, as though to signal I was saying more than she needed to know.

"Will he marry Teodora?" Nina yelled, seeing me on the edge of weeping. The woman took my hand again. "How many children will they have? Will he pass the final exam with flying colors?" the girls kept asking. "Sure he will. He's the best."

She looked at the outer side of my hand, near the pinky.

"You are strongly ruled by fate. Bigger forces than your own will are at work. Something will happen and you'll never go to college."

"Yep, we got finals coming up," I said, removing my hand from her grip. "I'm pretty worried. We're all pretty worried."

The girls laughed uncontrollably.

"Stop that giggling in the back row right now," I said in a penetrating voice, imitating Ms. B, and all four of us burst like fireworks across the night sky.

The woman took off her glasses, pressing her forefinger against the crease between her brows.

I stood up. The whole thing irked me, she could tell.

"Can your hand lines change over time?" Nina asked quietly yet urgently, like there's a bear nearby.

"They can and they do. Your health, for example, can change or your life can take a whole new direction. Many factors determine the course of our lives—we just mustn't ignore the signs."

The woman touches the pearls on her crane-like neck, glances at the clock on the wall in what seems a reflex motion, tells us the session's over, she'll see us to the door. Asks what brings us there. We thought it would be a cool destination for our graduation trip. The teachers couldn't say no. She looks as if she's sampling the wine, moving it around in her mouth. It's sour.

***

"C'mon," Nina said in an attempt to talk me into it, and I gave her a thin smile. "C'mon," she went on begging, then others chimed in with "those who live like cowards die a cowardly death" and "the brave die but once," "c'mon," ringing like trumpets on the street parade. "C'mon, you can't say no to me." She was right. I couldn't. So after a series of no's, I uttered a pale and unconvincing yes.

I'd known her for years. She reminded me of my sister—flamboyant in character, short and skinny as hell. Made me think she was running on air, though I never had the guts to tell her.

But it was more than that. It was like a piercing cry in the middle of a quiet night that called to me.

"I guess it could be fun," I said. Nina's mouth twisted into a smile of gleeful satisfaction. She was proud of her persuasion skills—there was no doubt about it.

Without further ado, she squared her shoulders and knocked her knuckles against the door before someone signaled at the button. I pressed it and the door unlocked automatically. A dead stillness fell on everything around us, unchanging and eternal like the last sleep, then a voice shrieked *straight on, I left the door ajar.* I felt like I had a loaded gun in my mouth, thought I could almost taste the metal. Hand in hand, we pushed it open and went in.

***

Ms. B, our history teacher, tapped the bus driver on the shoulder and he pulled over at the next stop. When we got off, we wandered down the crowded streets of Athens for hours, frittering away on whatever took our fancy, until Nina saw a palm reader sign, grabbed my hand and pulled me closer. We gazed fixedly at a pile of detached hands in the window, tried to understand. They reminded me of toddlers severed from their mothers, bunched together in unnatural clusters, gesticulating madly.

"Spooky!" I shouted, as if to overpower all the hustle and bustle around. Holding my hand with a firm grip, Nina lowered her voice to a low pitch. "Nah, it's more like a scary book daring you to read on."

I was unable to think for a while. Not sure I wanted to. Like a gun falling silent, I savored the moment—a break from an unwanted whistling inside.

Toys We've Outplayed, Books We're Sure We Won't Read Again

You just cleared the table and threw your stuffed animals in the washer, scrubbed and rinsed every item you set your heart on passing on to younger kids. *Conscientious already*, they say. It's not that. It itches, so you scratch. You make your bed, pick your brother's clothes up off the floor—do things without being asked.

Mid-school's pretty much the same. The skirts and pants you've outgrown you either give away or store in the attic—touch your belly, think of your children. You hang the sheets on the washing line, hang your jackets on a hook behind the door. You don't pack your closet with stuff you can't get in there or sleep in a tent because you're using your bed as a temporary storage for everything. You attribute it to age difference and gender—our brains differ after all.

In high school, you tear out magazine photos and articles, organize them into fun folders and files, pretty them up with scrapbook paper. You've got a project coming up— make art with magazine clippings based on who you are. *I'm so not sure I'm doing this right*, you think—*what if clipping doesn't do the job?*—then resort to Photoshop for modifications.

In college, you study hard to move away, never to go back, have your do's and don'ts, your will's and won'ts. (Don't throw things out the window when the world's come to an end. Use a self-motivational phrase quickly and repeatedly, almost as one word—keep it together, keepittogether, keepittogether.)

"How long would you stay with us?" the principal asks.

"As long as we both feel I'm contributing, thriving, growing."

You've got a job now, no children—honestly, who'd want children now (or ever with so many rascals around?) At work, you keep your belongings clean and ordered, arrange them in a systematic way. (You love the word *systematic*.) Your house is no different. The back of the closet is for storing seasonal clothing, topmost shelves for games you're not ready to play yet.

Your taste and favorites haven't changed—the colors stay neutral, floor is unscratched, furniture well taken care of. *She should've been a pharmacist*, they say. You love the way in which things are structured here, anywhere. And you love filing, making good use of every piece of newspaper you've ever read. If there's just one small item on a page you want to keep, you circle it so you know why you've kept it. Sometimes you make notes on the page—cool decorating ideas and stuff.

You're mature, do what mature people do, don't bitch when things don't go well. Your behavior is perceived as predictable, but that's ok. You've never liked surprises to start with.

You've fallen for someone. Didn't know you weren't supposed to until he said *let's try being adult about thi*s. Keepittogether, you're mature, keepittogether.

You're seeing another colleague, in another school, though, another town. He walks you home after work, shares his fries and views with you.

"No snacking," he says on a Friday afternoon, "we'll ruin dinner."

Next Friday, you ask him to come in for a drink when he notices your *thing*. You want to say it's like a small chip in a wine glass—you still want to keep it—you bite the rim, say it's your sick day activity. Fuck! He'll think you're sick way too often. But he says he keeps spreadsheets and printouts in binders, and you loosen up, run your fingers through your hair.

"I have a hard time tossing mags out, I have to cull through them in the end," you go on, eyes sparkling like a warm wave, asking him to ride it, embrace it. He looks all ready to seal the deal. "Same here," he says.

"Yeah?"

"Yeah. I cut out the best photos and put them in a book, although I'm not nearly as meticulous as you are."

Aw shucks, you think after he tells you he's saying that coz it's true. You can't stop the blood rushing to your face. When you wake up the next morning, you grin at each other, bellies pressed together.

The following week, he buys you a basket for magazines you're currently reading. The handles make it easy to move around. You feel fluffy, so fluffy you want to die. *I'm sensing he knows me*, you think. *I'm sensing he really knows me.*

"How long will you stay?" you ask a month from now.

"How long would you want me to stay?"

You may hit the wrong button, think before answering, think, think!

"As long as we both feel we're contributing, thriving, growing."

He stays.

With time, you're more selective about which journals to buy and which to keep since they've become rather expensive and hard to organize in chronological order, in any other order. Lots of times you simply walk into Barnes & Noble to browse through their stuff without feeling guilty.

You're middle-aged, and starting to feel awkward. *I'm sensing you don't know me, you don't me at all*, you think, seeing him throw out something he calls redundant before you go to the kitchen—that's where all the knives are. You watch your students taking notes, think how you hate teaching—all the grading you have to do, counting chickens before they hatch—think, cut yourself out of the photos of the two of you, hang the laundry out to dry, get divorce papers ready—there's nothing left we can do to each other—think, have your house redecorated (fall decorating ideas/ repair cost file).

When you retire, you knit sweaters, stitch around the neck to make a collar, miss a stitch or two. Your skin is dumb and prickly, feels like wool. You're looking at me. You're looking right at me. I'm the one with covers pulled up to her chin, fleshy and heavy, drained of all blood. The one you call *hey, you* and *that kind of woman*. I'm the one you stopped calling.

You think you know me? You think you really know me?

You think I'm nothing, not anything, no single thing. I will be—just not today. Today I am a future pile of dust, like you.

I'm starting to feel awkward. Do you feel awkward?

About the Author

Bojana Stojčić was born, raised and educated in Serbia / lived in Canada / lives in Germany where she teaches and writes. Starting a writer's blog back in 2017 reminded her how much she loves writing. As of then, dozens of her works of fiction, nonfiction, (prose) poetry, book reviews and essays have found beautiful homes in numerous literary journals, print and online magazines and anthologies, Rust + Moth, Anti-Heroin Chic, Barren Magazine, Ink Sweat & Tears, Versification and Okay Donkey, among others. She mainly writes women-centered stories in both realistic and magical settings, and loves dry humor, dark fiction and anti-heroism. This is her debut book.